THE SPANISH SAILOR

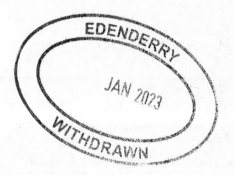

The Arts Council
An Chomhairle Ealaíon

The Publishers gratefully acknowledge the financial
assistance of The Arts Council/An Chomhairle Ealaíon

First published in 2001 by Mercier Press
5 French Church Street Cork
Tel: (021) 275040; Fax: (021) 274969
E-mail: books@mercier.ie
16 Hume Street Dublin 2
Tel: (01) 661 5299; Fax: (01) 661 8583
E-mail: books@marino.ie

Trade enquiries to CMD Distribution
55A Spruce Avenue
Stillorgan Industrial Park
Blackrock County Dublin
Tel: (01) 294 2556; Fax: (01) 294 2564
E.mail: cmd@columba.ie

© Bríd Mahon 2001
Illustrations © Cliodhna Quinlan 2001

ISBN 1 85635 367 2
10 9 8 7 6 5 4 3 2 1

A CIP record for this title is available
from the British Library

Cover design by Penhouse Design

Printed in Ireland by ColourBooks,
Baldoyle Industrial Estate, Dublin 13

THE SPANISH SAILOR

BRÍD MAHON

Illustrated by

CLIODHNA QUINLAN

MERCIER PRESS

for Rachel and David
and all the boys and girls who like a bit of magic

CONTENTS

1

THE SPANISH SAILOR

Since early morning the sun had been dancing over the rooftops of the city. It slanted across the window of a tall narrow house, waking Conor from a dream in which a mirror, his aunt Bee and a Spanish ship were all mixed up. He lay staring at the ceiling and thinking about his aunt. She was, in Conor's opinion, a very vain woman, dressing herself up in odd clothes, long skirts, gold earrings that reached to her shoulders and red hair which she scraped up on top of her head. Not like his mother, who dressed sensibly, as a mother should. She knew lots of tricks with cards and had more stories in her head than any book. She never asked for anything and was always surprised and delighted with any gift. Aunt Bee, on the other hand, had been dropping hints about her birthday ever since she arrived, telling Conor how she longed for a mirror that would show her things as they really were.

By the merest chance, Conor had discovered a mirror that just might do in a shop that was hidden away in a courtyard near his home. It was a rundown little place, the window crowded with junk of every sort: cracked teapots, rusty spoons, headless dolls and an old-fashioned sailing ship, torn and battered. The shop was the kind you would pass without a second glance, except for the hand mirror hidden away in one corner, bright and sparkling behind the dust. Chalked on the windowpane were the words:

No Reasonable Offer for Goods Refused

That night, Conor had taken all his savings out of the box, hidden under his bed, which contained his treasures. He hoped he had enough money to buy the mirror, and wondered what a 'reasonable offer' might mean.

Now the birthday had at last dawned, and he couldn't contain his impatience. Nothing stirred. His twin, Kathleen, and Aunt Bee were still fast asleep. He dressed as quickly as he could despite his limp and left the house, pulling the door quietly behind him. At the top of the road, he paused to watch a circus pass by – ponies with stars on their foreheads, ridden by girls in spangly dresses; a lion asleep in the corner of a rusty cage that creaked as it went past; a clown driving a splendid yellow caravan, followed by a line of carts and more caravans; and a lorry holding the canvas and poles that would make up the Big Top. Straggling along behind yet managing to keep up were a skinny red-haired boy and a fat man pulling a dog tied with a length of rope, a black-and-white dog with floppy ears and a coat matted with dirt. As the tail-end of the circus straggled past, Conor decided to count his money once more, watched closely by the red-haired boy and the fat man. They had come swaggering over to where he stood, barring his path when he tried to move away. 'Want to buy a well-bred dog used for winning prizes?' the fat man shouted. 'She's going cheap.'

Two mournful doggy eyes pleaded with Conor and a tail wagged hopefully. Conor was tempted. Then he shook his head. 'I can't. I have to buy my aunt a mirror for her birthday.'

The moment the words were out, he knew he had made a fool of himself. The pair fell around the place laughing. 'Listen to him!' they howled. 'He has to buy his auntie a present. Happy birthday, dear Auntie, happy birthday to you!'

Conor felt his temper rise: 'Leave me alone,' he shouted, trying to escape, but his limp slowed him up and by now the red-haired boy had him in a vicious grip.

'Not so fast, Hoppity. We have a few tricks to show you.'

The fat man jerked the rope, lifting the dog off the ground, so that the animal was in danger of choking. Now, even more than being called 'Hoppity', Conor hated to see an animal ill-treated, and besides, he had a fellow feeling for the poor dog. 'Leave her alone!' he shouted. 'Hasn't she got a name?'

'We call her Lightning.' The fat man screeched with laughter. 'She goes that fast.'

'She might if she wasn't nearly choked to death by that rope,' Conor said crossly. 'Where did you get her?'

The thin boy sighed. 'If only ye knew the whole sad story. There we was, going along, mindin' our own business, and this mongrel decides to folly us. We tried to teach her a few tricks to earn her keep in the circus, see, but she's too stupid to learn. If you don't buy her, we'll soon have to drown her or somefin'.'

In a panic, Conor handed over his money, but as if that wasn't enough, they rifled through his pockets, taking a conking chestnut, a magnifying glass, a pen that could write in two colours and a football badge. Then they were gone, and a cold wind blew down the street.

Conor untied the rope, and patted the dog. 'I'll look after you,' he promised, but she shook herself free and went galloping off in the direction taken by her tormentors.

A woman with a shopping bag paused to sympathise with Conor. 'A pair of rogues. They must try that trick on with every kind-hearted person they meet. They have their dog well trained.'

Conor was too disheartened to tell anyone what had happened. He walked along kicking stones, then suddenly remembered he had had no breakfast, and turned back towards home. In the kitchen, Kathleen was putting the finishing touches to a silver shell made to hold a string of blue beads. 'You have a face on you that would stop a clock,' she chided. 'Maybe you're sickening for measles. Aunt Bee will give you a dose and send you to bed.'

Conor put out his tongue and just had enough time to withdraw it before Aunt Bee came floating into the room as if her feet weren't on the ground at all. He watched moodily as she toasted crumpets and cooked bacon and sausages, which were normally his favourite breakfast. This morning he couldn't care less.

'I have decided to postpone the celebration of my birthday until suppertime,' Aunt Bee announced to the room at large. 'I must admit I am looking forward to my presents. It is amazing what one can hear in a silver seashell, and blue beads will match my eyes. The golden mirror, too, will come in useful. Besides, now that the circus has left town, it's about time the dog was found.'

'Wha' circus? Wha' dog?' Kathleen's mouth was full of sausage and she couldn't speak properly. 'Will someone please tell me wha's goin' on, thass all I ask?'

'And all I ask,' her aunt said crisply, 'is that you refrain from speaking with your mouth full. No doubt Conor will explain all in his own good time.'

Conor didn't feel like explaining anything, and his aunt's remarks made him feel even more fed up, if that were possible. Without finishing his breakfast or excusing himself, he got up from the table and went out of the room, banging the door behind him.

'If only Dad and Mum were here, they would give me enough money to buy the mirror,' he thought miserably, but his parents were archaeologists, excavating a Pharaoh's tomb in faraway Egypt, while he and Kathleen spent the summer holidays with their aunt.

As he walked away from the house, he had a feeling that the road was keeping up with him, then taking over and finally leading him down the alleyway and into the courtyard where the odd little shop stood. Standing before the window was the black-and-white dog he had rescued – the selfsame dog, wagging her tail for all she was worth.

She had run away from him, yet he was delighted to see her again. She looked so eager and excited and friendly. He bent down to stroke her floppy ears and she nudged him playfully, so that he tumbled backwards, banging his head against the window ledge. For a moment, stars danced before his eyes. When they cleared, he found that everything had changed. The window was clean and the glass clear and sparkling, filled with a magician's wand, a witch's hat, a crystal ball, a china pig and a golden three-legged pot filled with gold coins. Of all the junk that had filled the window the day before, only the golden mirror remained, now holding pride of place in the centre. A message written in chalk on the glass read:

A Good Price Given for a Healthy Dog Named Flash
Do Come In and That Means YOU

Excitedly, Conor pushed the door open, followed closely by the dog.

'Close the door after you,' a voice ordered. Conor did as he was told.

'Come closer.' The voice appeared to come from a white egg behind the counter. Conor came closer. It wasn't an egg at all, but the bald pate of a little fat man. As Conor leaned across the counter, the little man climbed up onto a stool. 'Well, my boy, and what do you want?' he demanded. 'I'm not selling anything today, and that's flat.' His voice was high and sharp, like the wind in the rushes.

'I – I saw a message in your window,' Conor began. 'About a dog lost, strayed or stolen.'

'Most likely the last,' the little man said. 'Well, what do you know about her?'

Before Conor could answer, Flash leaped onto the counter. The effect on the little man was extraordinary. He clapped his hand to his forehead and said in a shaking voice, 'You mean to say you had Flash all the time, and we searching for her?'

Conor was puzzled. 'Is Flash her name? The red-haired boy and the fat man said it was Lightning.'

'You're not by any chance in league with them?' the little man asked, scowling. 'I suspect they stole Flash.'

'They stole all my money and other things too,' Conor said crossly. 'Anyhow, if she belongs to you, there's no more to be said.'

The little man reached into the window and picked up the mirror. He pushed it across the counter. 'We promised a fair exchange. Take it or leave it.'

Conor saw that the mirror was cracked and tarnished. He turned on his heel and almost bumped into a sailor boy, who hadn't been there before. The boy might have been expected to explain himself or even to pass the time of day, he thought. Long after the adventure was over, Conor would remember the dusty shop, the cross little man and Flash with her head cocked to one side while the sailor boy sang in a foreign accent:

I am a Spanish sailor boy
And I come from a far countr-ee
I've treasure, map and Spanish gold
And a little orange tree.

I came to Ireland long ago
In a galleon tall and brave
We struck a rock in the Blasket Sound
And sank beneath a wave.

When the north wind blows a hurricane
And the waves are very high
Then perhaps you'll see the Spanish ship
And the ghost of the Spanish boy.

In the shop, something very strange was happening. The walls were closing in and the sailor boy was nothing more than a shadow. The little man with the egg-shaped head had vanished. Only the dog, wagging her tail, looked real.

Afterwards, Conor could never remember how he got out of the shop. He didn't draw breath until he was safely inside his front door. It all might have been a dream, except for the tarnished mirror he was tightly clutching in his hand. 'I'll go back to the shop and ask for the three-legged pot of gold or the crystal ball instead,' Conor decided. 'I wish I had never parted with Flash so easily.'

Yet the odd thing was that although he spent the rest of the day searching, he could not find the

'I am a Spanish sailor boy and I come from a far countr-ee'

alleyway again, let alone the shop. In the end, he gave up and set out for home.

It had been a queer, mixed-up day, and he was glad to turn into the road where he lived and see the tall thin house, looking the same as ever. While no one was around, he slid the mirror under a heap of presents at his aunt's place at table. Sometimes Aunt Bee was easygoing, occasionally she was severe and almost always she was unpredictable. At the birthday tea, she was in high good humour and everything pleased her. She blew out the candles in one breath and cut the cake into thick slices, pronouncing it delicious. Then, at last, she turned her attention to the heap of birthday gifts. Top of the pile was a diamond-shaped bottle with a glass stopper, filled with a curious liquid that constantly changed colour. 'All the way from your parents in Egypt,' she announced, and read out the birthday message: 'We got this from a magician in a bazaar in Cairo. You can smell whatever you like best.'

She unscrewed the stopper and took a deep and satisfying breath. 'Oranges and sawdust in a circus ring. How very intriguing.' Conor got a distinct aroma of roasted chestnuts and chips, while for Kathleen, it was the unmistakeable smell of burnt toffee and pancakes.

Aunt Bee replaced the stopper and opened Kathleen's gift next. With an elegant gesture, she fastened the blue beads around her neck and held the silver shell to her ear. 'More than anything else, I long to hear the sound of the sea,' she said. 'I recognise the very place this shell was found and I fully intend to go there very soon.'

'I wish she's hurry up and get it over,' Conor muttered, watching impatiently while his aunt held up the mirror, which looked even more battered and useless. Before she could stop herself, Kathleen blurted out: 'What an extraordinary present to give you.'

Aunt Bee looked down her nose at her niece. 'Naturally. I *am* an extraordinary woman, and hardly expected anything commonplace.'

Kathleen said nothing. For once in her life, she couldn't think of an answer to make. Conor sat scowling nervously while his aunt studied her face in the mirror. Then she pushed the mirror across the table. 'Well, Conor, and what do you see?'

At first he could see nothing. Then, like frost on a window when the sun comes out, the cloud on the glass was melting away. What was staring back at him was not his own face, but the face of the Spanish sailor.

Impatiently, Kathleen snatched the mirror. 'I see a black-and-white dog wagging her tail.'

'That will be Flash. Nothing to get excited about.'

Very coolly, Aunt Bee took back the mirror and sat staring into it. This time, neither Conor nor Kathleen could wait. They were around the table, looking over their aunt's shoulder even before the glass had changed.

It was like watching television or a film. A green, latticed gate swung open into a long garden where a grey donkey was browsing, while a black-and-white dog chewed a bone. In the centre of the garden stood an orange tree, and at the far end, a thatched cottage. A dark-haired sailor boy was peeping out through a window.

'I met him today in a shop,' Conor burst out. 'I had an adventure.'

Kathleen clutched his arm dramatically. 'Tell me all. Mind and leave nothing out.'

And Conor did tell her. And when he had finished, the picture faded away and the glass clouded over once more.

There was a faraway look in Aunt Bee's eyes and a nostalgic note in her voice as she said: 'No mirror can show what it is really like; the magic is in the air. The horseshoe beach at Coumeenole and the Blasket Islands, the circus, the dolphin, the enchanted cave, the divers and the Spanish treasure at the bottom of the Blasket Sound. Yes, indeed, I have made up my mind and nothing anyone can say will make me change it. Tomorrow I intend to go and take you both with me. It is the only possible thing to do.'

And so it was that early next morning they piled into her little blue car and drove out of town. They followed the great main road until it gave way to smaller roads and finally took one that wound over the mountains and dropped down to the sea. Night had fallen as they rounded Slea Head on the outermost edge of the Dingle Peninsula, and the moon cut a silver path across the waters to where the islands lay, dark and remote.

And that very night they slept in the white cottage they had first seen in the broken mirror and where so much was to happen in the weeks to come.

2

THE BALLAD SINGER

The cottage had whitewashed walls and a thatched roof, and the rooms were oddly shaped. In the garden, an old tree that was leafless and bent with age changed colour with every wind that blew. Conor and Kathleen had never seen its like before although Big Tom, the fisherman who was their nearest neighbour, swore it was a tree from Spai: 'Planted by a young prince, hundreds of years ago. He left it to remind people he was once here.'

The sea road went past in front of the cottage, and on the far side were fields and a stretch of water that divided the mainland from the Blasket Islands. Around the islands, the wide Atlantic stretched ceaselessly westwards.

Aunt Bee had always been odd and mysterious, but never more so than that summer. She tied the laces of her shoes around her ankles, as if she was afraid they would fly away when she wasn't looking. When she sneezed, she could conjure up a handkerchief out of thin air. Some days she dressed in sensible shoes and skirts and made them eat good nourishing meals – porridge and stew, fresh eggs and lots of milk. Other days, and for no particular reason, she dressed like a gypsy, wearing colourful skirts and red shoes. At times like these they had pancakes for breakfast, sausages and chips for lunch and all the ice cream they could manage. She was an artist, and hung the walls of the cottage with paintings of Irish castles and Spanish squares thronged with people. At night, when the firelight made shapes, it seemed as if the pictures were alive and the painted people might step into the room at any moment.

When the weather was fine, the twins went down to the pier to help Big Tom bring in the catch. 'I was reared on the Great Blasket Island,' he told them. 'Now the place is deserted, though my old home is still there, same as the day I left.' He was sitting with his back to the harbour wall, mending a net and whistling a tune.

'A sailor boy I once met in a queer little shop knew that tune,' Conor said thoughtfully. He was reminded of his strange experience by the song Big Tom was whistling. 'There was a little man with a bald head, and I swapped a dog for a mirror to give to my aunt for a birthday present.'

'Nothing will shake my belief that the sailor boy was a ghost,' Kathleen said. She was perched on an upturned currach, swinging her legs. 'Also, I'm as sure as anything that the little bald man was a leprechaun.'

'Maybe you're right,' Big Tom agreed. 'My friend the ballad singer says the little fellows have been around for thousands of years. They make and mend shoes and have crocks of gold hidden away that no mortal can ever find.'

'What did I tell you?' In her excitement, Kathleen

tumbled off the currach. She nudged Conor. 'Go on, tell him what happened.'

'The sailor boy appeared out of nowhere. He sang a song like the tune you've just been whistling.' Conor could only remember the last verse:

When the north wind blows a hurricane
And the waves are very high
Then perhaps you'll see the Spanish ship
And the ghost of the Spanish boy.

Big Tom kept time with his foot. 'My friend the ballad singer knows that song very well. I'd lay a bet he knows every ballad there ever was. Oh, 'tis he had the life. Brought up in a castle, no less, like a lord. Then he got tired of it all and took to the roads. Now you'll hear him at every fair, parade, race meeting and gathering in the country.'

Kathleen sighed. 'It is my one great wish to meet a lord. Next to that, I'd like to meet a ballad singer.'

'One of these days, you will,' Big Tom promised. 'Over the mountains he'll come, in a fine black coat and a long white beard. Oh, 'tis himself will tell Conor of the sailor boy whose ghost roams these parts looking for a thing he hid a long while back.'

'My aunt is a firm believer in ghosts,' Kathleen declared. 'Moreover, I have a feeling in my bones that Mount Eagle is haunted.'

'You're always imagining things,' Conor sniffed. Yet he couldn't help wondering. That night, beside the fire, he told Aunt Bee all of Big Tom's story.

Aunt Bee pulled out a strand of her hair, twisted it around her little finger, and shook out a long red scarf, which she then draped around her head. 'Many strange events have happened around Mount Eagle,' she agreed thoughtfully. 'A heap of stones near the top marks the spot where the Spanish sailor is buried. On the far side is Ventry Strand, where Finn MacCool and his warriors had their headquarters, thousands of years ago. Finn was the wisest man in Ireland because he ate the Salmon of Knowledge and Caelte MacRonan was the champion runner. He could go faster than the wind.'

'I wish I could run like Caelte,' Conor muttered, gazing into the flames and seeing pictures of a boy running along the strand while the crowds of the world cheered him on. He never admitted it to a living soul, but he hated being lame, hated coming last in every race, and longed to play on a football team.

Aunt Bee looked as if she could read his thoughts. 'Always remember, Conor,' she said, 'that if you want a thing badly enough, you're bound to get it in the end. If not, something even better is sure to turn up.'

And the next morning it did. It was Midsummer's Eve to begin with, the most magical day of the year. When night fell, bonfires would blaze from every mountain and hilltop in Ireland. The twins had just finished breakfast when Big Tom arrived, leading a small grey donkey with long ears. 'Here's a likely lad for ye. Over on the headlands near Coumeenole I found him with a pack of bold wild donkeys.'

Kathleen stroked the donkey's long ears. 'He's a dote. What will we call him?'

Big Tom chuckled. 'Sure, he brought his name with him – Long Ears.'

Aunt Bee gave the donkey a sugar lump, the twins climbed up on his back, Big Tom gave his rump a pat, and they were away up a boreen behind the cottage.

The road led up the cloudy mountain. Big Tom's cottage was near the top and they saw a black-and-white dog chasing sheep. 'It reminds me of Flash,' Conor said, 'but, sure, it couldn't be the same dog.'

Clip, clip went the donkey's hooves over the rough ground. 'Caw, caw,' cried a golden eagle flying over-head.

Long Ears made a sudden leap over a stone wall and the twins shot up in the air, coming down on a thorn bush. When they picked themselves up and dusted themselves down, the donkey had vanished, and the place was lonely and silent once more.

'I'm full of prickles,' Kathleen grumbled. She noticed her brother was limping worse than ever. 'Did you hurt your foot?'

Conor pretended not to hear. He hopped over a mound of stones. 'Here's a broken headstone. Listen to what it says: "Here lie the last mortal remains of the Spanish sailor. He will not rest until he finds that which he seeks."'

Kathleen shivered. 'I knew the minute I set foot in this place it was haunted.'

Wind was blowing the mist away and storm clouds were gathering overhead. A clap of thunder echoed around the mountains and a flash of lightning tore across the sky. It reminded Conor of the little black-and-white dog and he wondered would he ever see her again.

Far below in the Blasket Sound an old-fashioned sailing ship was rounding the great island. As they stood, mesmerised, the ship keeled over and sank beneath the waves.

'The Spanish ship,' Conor breathed.

'A ghost,' Kathleen wailed. She took to her heels. 'I'm going home.'

'Wait for me,' Conor howled, hopping along on one foot. 'You know well I can't keep up.'

Gusts of wind swept the face of the mountain, his foot hurt, and he couldn't see where he was going. He found Kathleen crouched behind a rock. 'I wish we had never come up here,' she sobbed.

'I'll whistle and maybe Long Ears will hear me.' Conor put two fingers in his mouth and blew hard. They waited. Then, unbelievably, a wet, bedraggled little black-and-white dog came hurtling towards them. 'It's Flash,' Conor said.

'No wonder they call her Flash, if she goes that fast,' Kathleen said, patting the little mongrel on the head, but the dog wriggled away and was gone, bounding through a thicket of furze.

'Follow her,' Conor urged. 'You're able to run faster than me.'

Kathleen wouldn't budge. 'I'll only lose you. I'll stay here and we'll perish together, and they'll find our bodies beside the grave of the Spanish sailor.'

'Stuff and nonsense,' Conor growled. He could hear movements nearby – leaves crackling, mud squelching and hooves pattering.

A bearded man in a long black coat was coming

The Ballad Singer

around the bend with Flash at his heels and Long Ears trotting docilely behind. He doffed his battered hat in a courtly bow. 'Please allow me to introduce myself. I am the Ballad Singer, at your service.'

Kathleen beamed through her tears. 'Big Tom told us all about you.'

'I was taking a short cut over the mountains when the storm broke,' the Ballad Singer said. 'I took shelter in a beehive hut and discovered this fine dog sheltering in the same spot.'

'I thought she belonged to a little man I met in a shop,' Conor began, but the Ballad Singer shook his head. 'I'd say she belongs to herself, though now and again she's apt to wander.' He swung the twins up on the donkey's back.

'I think you have had enough adventure for one day. The sooner we make tracks for home, the better.'

Kathleen bounced up and down. 'We had a truly fantastic time,' she boasted. 'We came across the grave of the Spanish sailor and saw the ghost of the Spanish ship.'

'And I found Flash again,' Conor said happily.

'Or maybe Flash found you.' The Ballad Singer winked at Conor. 'I don't want to say too much just now. As you know, walls have ears, and a certain pair from the circus may be somewhere around. All the same, I have a feeling that particular events are about to take place and that the hunt for the Spanish treasure is well and truly under way.'

3

THE GREAT BLASKET ISLAND

An early-morning mist covered the peninsula, giving the promise of a lovely day. On the headlands above Coumeenole a grey donkey with long ears kicked his heels and raced down a steep path to a hidden cove, watched by a dolphin basking in the bay. A seabird flew overhead with a raucous cry, and the dolphin wheeled around in the clear water, striking out for the big island.

From the door of the white cottage, the twins watched as the Ballad Singer went whistling along the sea road with Flash at his heels. Behind came Big Tom playing his flute. The twins waved cheerfully and he waved back.

'Wish I was going with them,' muttered Conor. He was fitting a new battery into his torch. He tested the light and slipped the torch into his pocket.

'Time for breakfast,' Aunt Bee sang out. This morning they were having fried trout and mushrooms, followed by croissants spread with blueberry jam, and the table was colourful, with a bowl of wild roses on it. Aunt Bee was wearing golden hoops in her ears and her scarlet wool skirt had bands of black velvet around the hem.

'When I was in America,' she confided, cupping her chin with her hands and leaning across the table, 'I went to a rodeo show and rode a bucking bronco. No one could stay on his back but me. I was crowned Queen of the Rodeo and was presented with these gold earrings you see me wearing. I met the last Red Indian in the Californian backwoods. He was a prince and I was tempted to invite him back to Ireland but I had second thoughts. The climate wouldn't be to his liking.'

'Was he wearing feathers in his hair? Was his face painted?' Kathleen demanded.

Aunt Bee smiled. 'He would have caused something of a sensation walking down O'Connell Street beating a drum.'

'Enough to cause a traffic jam,' Conor put in, his mouth full of blueberry preserves.

The twins were never sure whether Aunt Bee's stories were true or make-believe, but there was no denying the fact that she had run away with the circus when she was young and had gone travelling the world. 'I was looking for something I could never find,' she said with a faraway look in her eyes. 'On the other hand, if you went to the Great Blasket you might just be lucky.'

'I'm longing to go,' Conor said wistfully.

'And I have constantly hinted to Big Tom to take us,' Kathleen added. 'But my words have fallen on deaf ears.'

Aunt Bee took a picnic basket from the top of the dresser. 'By a strange coincidence, Big Tom told me he was going lobster-fishing this very morning. He suggested you should accompany him. I have a lunch basket packed and ready, so there should be no delay.'

'What are we waiting for?' Conor shouted, and was out the door as fast as his legs could carry him.

Kathleen put on her sunglasses to impress Big Tom and, swinging her basket, she followed her brother down the sea road.

Fishing nets were spread across the rocks at the pier and the newly tarred currachs lay upside down on the ground. Though the morning was hot, Big Tom was wearing his fisherman's jersey and his cap was back to front. The Ballad Singer had tied a red silk handkerchief around his head like a pirate captain. Flash ran around, chasing any birds who were fool-hardy enough to come down in search of fish.

'We were waiting for you,' Big Tom said cheerfully, and he and the Ballad Singer swung the currach up over their heads and marched down to the slip, looking for all the world like a giant beetle. As soon as they were all safely settled, Big Tom pushed out the boat, then jumped in himself. And they were off.

The boat swept gracefully along the coastline, around the headlands of Dún Mór, where the wild donkeys were racing each other. Then the lifting prow of the boat turned westwards and went skimming over the water. The mist had vanished and the sun sparkled on the islands. Inisicileáin, Inis na Bró and Beiginis were all flat and green, sheltering the smallest island, called Oileán na nÓg, the Island of Youth. They could see the Great Blasket, and further on still Inis Tuaisceart and the gull-haunted pyramid of the Tiaracht, where once the lighthouse flashed out a warning for passing ships.

'Long ago, people thought the Blaskets were on the edge of the world,' Big Tom told them. 'Then a fierce great traveller called Brendan the Navigator set out. He was gone close on seven years, and when he returned home, he told stories of a strange land he had visited, where Red Indians hunted the buffalo and the deer. Hundreds of years later, Christopher Columbus sailed to the same land, which is known today as America.'

Kathleen trailed her hand in the water and boasted, 'My aunt is a much-travelled woman. She knows America inside out. I am convinced she is a witch.'

Conor snorted. He didn't believe in such rubbish, but Kathleen couldn't be stopped. 'She knew we were lost on the mountains last night and could tell us what had happened when we got home. She knew the Ballad Singer rescued us.' Flash barked and Conor pulled her ears. 'You're a good girl. You found us.' He grinned at the Ballad Singer. 'Big Tom said you know all about the Spanish sailor and the treasure.'

'He does surely.' Big Tom rested his oars. 'He might as well tell you now as another time.'

The Ballad Singer pulled on his long white beard. 'It happened hundreds of years ago when the Spanish ships set out to fight Elizabeth the red-haired English queen. A great sight it was entirely – the Spanish Armada, they called it. But they were unlucky. No sooner had they reached the English Channel than a storm blew up, scattering the ships. A magnificent galleon, the *Santa Maria de la Rosa,* limped into these very waters you see before you. She struck Stromboli Rock under the cliffs, keeled over and sank.'

Conor leaned over the currach and peered into the depths. Here the currents were very strong. He could almost see the ship capsizing and coming to rest on the ocean bed, her sails all crumpled and torn. 'Did anyone live to tell the tale?'

'Only one Spanish sailor survived. He was taken as a prisoner to Dingle town, where he told a strange story claiming he was the King of Spain's son and that a fortune in gold bullion had gone down with the ship. He escaped and was hidden by the people around here, but the hardship he had endured was too much and he died soon after. His body was buried on top of Mount Eagle. His ghost is said to haunt these parts ever since, looking for something he can never find.'

When the Ballad Singer had finished his story, he dipped his oars and the boat cut through the water. Now they were passing the little islands and moving along the high front of the Great Blasket itself. Into the harbour the currach ran, then it turned on her axis and floated easily up to the slip. Big Tom secured the boat and Flash was the first to jump out. Big Tom lifted the picnic basket on his head and the Ballad Singer took a tin whistle out of his pocket and struck up a tune. With Flash leading the way, they marched around by the cliff, singing:

> *'Twas a comical sight that I saw by the sea*
> *An eel with a pipe and he playing to me*

An oyster so big and he dancing a jig
While the trout sang 'the top o' the morning'.

A house on the lee side of the island had whitewashed
walls and a thatched roof held down by ropes. Big
Tom lifted the latch and they all trooped inside. He
put the basket on a table scrubbed milky-white and
took off his cap. 'This is the house where I was born.
A hundred thousand welcomes to you.'

A dresser was filled with shining delft, an open
hearth was piled with turf and a ladder led to a loft
where fishing tackle was stored.

'I must admit, this is a very tasty house.' Kathleen
looked around in admiration.

'You'd think it was made of gingerbread,' Conor
mocked.

Kathleen sniffed and tossed back her hair. Then
she began to unpack the basket, calling out as she
placed the food on the table: 'Roast chicken and ham,
brown bread and gingerbread, a packet of dates, four
apples, a bottle of milk, a bag of sugar, another of tea
and a slab of currant cake.' She appealed to Big Tom.
'You must admit, my aunt is a very well-meaning
person.'

'That she is,' he agreed, setting a light to the fire
and working a bellows while Conor fetched water from
a nearby well.

For a while the only sound to be heard was the
rattle of knives and forks and spoons as they finished
the contents of the basket. Flash, chewing a bone under
the table, was soon asleep. When she awoke, Big Tom

was making plans to gather up the lobster pots. She came out wagging her tail but the Ballad Singer shook his head. 'You're to stay here and take care of Conor and Kathleen. Be sure they don't end up on the back of a dolphin.'

Conor pricked his ears. 'I'd like to meet one.'

'The cliffs are dangerous places, fit only for goats,' said Big Tom.

'Did you say goats or ghosts?' Kathleen squealed. 'Is the place haunted?'

'No self-respecting ghost would dream of appearing in daylight,' the Ballad Singer said, pulling his beard. 'Besides, we'll be back to collect the pair of you long before sunset.'

'We'll be looking for Kathleen, and she dazzling us with sight of her grand sunglasses,' Big Tom added. Laughing to himself, he went up to the loft to fetch fishing tackle. Then the two of them set out for the harbour.

Kathleen washed the dishes and Conor swept the floor with a heather broom, and when everything was tidied away, they went out, closing the door behind them. Flash was lying in a pool of sunshine. Conor rolled her over with his foot and she got up, wagging her tail. She jumped over a low stone wall and they began to climb to the summit of the island.

At the top, Conor flung himself down on the grass. 'We'll take a breather,' he said. On either side the cliffs dropped sharply away. From where they sat, they could see a motorboat making for the harbour. Kathleen closed her eyes and was soon asleep, dreaming she was taking a ride on the back of the dolphin. When she awoke, the sun had moved over the cove. The dolphin was enjoying the last of the warmth.

'Where's Flash?' Kathleen asked, getting to her feet.

'She was here a few minutes ago and now she's gone,' Conor said grumpily. 'That dog is always running away.' Then he was sorry and began to hunt around. He heard a whimper and parted a clump of bushes. Flash was rolled up in a ball. Conor caught her by the back of her neck. 'Come along, old girl. We're not playing hide and seek.'

Kathleen said, 'She's frightened or something.' Suddenly they became aware of loud voices nearby, and kept very quiet. Somewhere an argument was going on: 'If I lay hands on those kids, I'll throw them over the cliff, so help me.'

'Just as well the others are out fishing. Anyway, why do you want the dog back?'

The voices were coming nearer. One was shouting,

'Don't be more stupid than you can help. You know the oul' rhyme as well as I do.' And the voice began to intone in a lugubrious manner:

'High on the mountain the thunder rolls
Two children lost and a plot unfolds
A four-legged friend and a singer bold
They'll meet and discover the Spanish gold.'

'An' the four-legged friend is the oul' mongrel Flash. Anyway, it's all your fault, sellin' her to the young fella. We could do with the gold.'

Conor peeped out of their hiding place and saw the red-haired boy and the fat man arriving at the summit.

'I tell ye I'm all in.' The fat man was mopping his face.

'Yer always complainin'. A lazy pig, that's what ye are,' the red-haired boy hissed.

'Pu'rup your hands and I'll fight ye,' roared his companion. Flash began to bark frantically. Conor tried to quieten her, but it was too late.

'Jus' looka who's hidin' here.' The red-haired boy pulled the bushes apart and stood staring at them. 'Hoppity himself and his skinny sister and the oul' mongrel.'

'Tha's no dog,' the fat man grinned. 'Tha's a flash of greased lightning.'

Between them they dragged Flash out into the open. One had her head and the other her hind legs. They ran to the cliff's edge, swinging her back and forwards, shouting, 'Up she goes, over she rolls.'

'Let go of her!' Conor shouted. He threw himself on the red-haired boy and Flash wriggled free. The next minute, she had disappeared over the cliff.

Kathleen screamed and Conor said in a terrible voice, 'You've killed our dog.' He lay on the edge of the cliff and looked down. Far below, he could just make out Flash huddled on a ledge that jutted out over the sea. 'Take it easy, old girl, I'll rescue you.' His voice was carried away by the wind. Behind him, the red-haired boy and the fat man were blaming each other. 'Now we're in real trouble. It's all your fault, fatty.'

'It was you let go of her. The oul' Ballad Singer'll murder us when he finds out.'

Kathleen had discovered a goat track down the face of the cliff. She called to Conor. 'Over here!' Cautiously, they made their way down, feeling for footholds. They didn't dare look down, though they could hear Flash whimpering.

'We've made it,' Kathleen said breathlessly, and jumped onto the ledge beside Flash. Part of the cliff seemed to give way and Conor went hurtling past her. Kathleen caught at his coat and then she too was tumbling through the air. Incredibly, the pair of them landed on the back of the dolphin that was waiting in the little cove under the cliffs. Flash had climbed up onto a strip of shingle and seemed none the worse for wear. Conor and Kathleen gingerly slid off the back of the dolphin and clambered onto dry ground. Pipits, wheatears and a black-backed gull circulated excitedly overhead while Conor took his bearings. They were on a tiny beach, encircled by great rocks. There was no way back.

Flash disappeared into an opening and Conor remembered thankfully that he had pocketed his torch. He pressed the switch and followed Flash into the cave, with Kathleen timidly coming behind. Seaweed was piled high in it and the floor and walls were green. Flash whimpered excitedly. Conor waded deeper into the cave and aimed the beam of light above the little dog's head. 'Kathleen, there are pictures on the wall, some of them worn away,' he said.

It was obvious they had been made with great effort

The Red-haired Boy and the Fat Man

with a sharp instrument – a knife, or the edge of a stone. One picture showed the rough outline of a ship keeling over into the sea. Next was a matchstick man swimming away. A third showed him lying in a state of exhaustion on the beach. The next image was a beehive hut – they were very old buildings, but there were still dozens of them around the peninsula – and lastly there was a drawing of a dolphin, and another of a dog that resembled Flash. Conor screwed up his eyes. 'There was a message of some kind here, but the words are worn away,' he said.

Kathleen shivered. 'Was it the Spanish sailor?'

Conor nodded. 'Who else?'

Water was creeping over the floor, sucking the stones, washing around their ankles. Soon the cave would be submerged. Flash whimpered and ran outside. Conor gave a last look round the cave, but apart from the carvings on the wall there was no sign that a dark-haired sailor boy had hidden there so long ago.

A white fog was rolling in, smelling of damp salt and seaweed, as they stood at the edge of the sea, which was churning and sweeping over their feet and legs. They climbed on a rock and shouted for help while Flash threw back her head and howled to the sky. Beyond the rock the dolphin snorted and swam away.

Then, across the sea, a voice was calling, and out of the mist the currach appeared, looking grey and insubstantial.

'Big Tom to the rescue!' Kathleen shouted.

'And the Ballad Singer with him,' Conor said gleefully.

Big Tom steered the boat between the rocks and Flash made a flying leap, landing in the prow.

'How did you find us?' Kathleen demanded as soon as they were all safely settled on board.

The Ballad Singer gave a sigh of relief. 'As we were making for the harbour, a motorboat passed us. The red-haired boy and the fat man shouted that you were drowned at sea. Since then we've been searching. We thought it was all up when the mist came down.'

Big Tom swung the currach around. 'We're all right now. I know these waters like the back of my hand.'

The Ballad Singer smiled. 'A friend of yours helped. The dolphin showed us the way and we searching. Tell me, Kathleen, did you see any trace of a ghost?'

'Just wait till you hear,' the twins chorused, and as the boat cut across to the mainland, they told them all that had happened and of the last lonely message the sailor had left in the Cave of the Dolphins.

4

A Wily Fox

A gust of wind blew down the chimney, making the sparks dance and lighting up the green eyes of the china pig that sat on the mantelpiece. It reminded Aunt Bee of something that had happened a long time ago. 'I was going to a fair and I met a pig with a star on its forehead. It could dance on its trotters and whistle a tune. I truly suspect it wasn't an ordinary pig.'

Kathleen sniffed scornfully. She didn't much care for pigs. Aunt Bee was knitting a white wool cap. She cast off the last stitch. 'I call this a Considering Cap. If Kathleen should take it into her head to go mushroom picking some fine morning, I strongly advise her to wear this cap.' She put her knitting wool and needles into a holdall and arranged the cap on top of the tin can used for blackberry picking and mushroom gathering. Then she turned her attention to Conor. 'I once knew a jockey who rode a pig in the Derby, and won the race too.'

Conor grinned. 'That must have been worth the watching.'

'Make no mistake it was,' Aunt Bee said, poking the

fire. 'On the other hand, a fox is a horse of a different colour, as my grandmother used to say. A certain fox has his den in the mountains behind this very cottage. He can take you anywhere in the world you wish to go. You have only to take hold of the tail and say where.'

Conor wondered where he would go if he had a wish – to Egypt to see his parents dig up a Pharaoh's tomb, or maybe to meet Finn MacCool and especially Caelte the champion runner, or best of all to meet the Spanish sailor. 'I wish I knew him,' he muttered.

No one was paying any attention to him. Kathleen had fallen asleep in the chair and Aunt Bee was humming softly to herself. The flames cast dancing shadows on the walls, and the glowing coals in the fire made shapes: a shining castle, a ship with tall riggings sailing a stormy sea. In years to come, Conor would remember that night and Aunt Bee's voice as she sang:

Once I had an orange tree, a golden chain, a ring,
A sword my father gave to me, sing merry ship-
mates, sing!

Once I sailed the seven seas, for I was brave as most,
Then our ship was cruelly wrecked, and I became a
ghost.

Once I owned, and then I left, a castle tall in Spain,
Oh help me find that which I seek, sing shipmates,
sing again.

That night, in his dreams, Conor climbed the orange tree in the garden. Then the dream changed and he was on a moonlit road. His limp was gone and he was running, swift as the wind. He knew this was the island road and that somewhere around him, the Spanish treasure was hidden. A crowd was coming up behind him. He saw the red-haired boy from the circus and the fat man, the leprechaun he had met in the odd little shop riding a pig and a fox with a bushy tail. 'We're going to the circus,' they all chorused, and the leprechaun caught his arm. When he turned, Aunt Bee was beside him. She was shaking him awake, saying 'Rise and shine.'

'I was dreaming about a circus,' he told her, yawning.

She laughed. 'You must have heard me in your sleep. I was just telling you that the circus has arrived in the village.'

With a bound, Conor was out of bed and in an instant had forgotten all about his dream.

At breakfast, Aunt Bee sat at the top of the table and poured tea from a fat brown teapot. 'Did you know,' she said, 'that some potted plants relish a drop of tea? Some even thrive on tea leaves.'

'Hee-haw,' Long Ears brayed in agreement. He had already finished his morning feed of carrots and turnip tops and laid his head on the ledge of the open window, the better to hear Aunt Bee. She ignored the interruption and continued her discourse. 'It is a well-established fact that blackcurrants like blackcurrant wine and that cowslips fancy cow's milk. Likewise, orange trees enjoy orange juice.'

Kathleen wondered what whin bushes fancied. She was convinced that the yellow blossoms tasted of bread and cheese. Conor chewed solidly on his bacon and thought about the circus.

When they had finished eating, Aunt Bee filled a watering can from a tin of orange juice. 'Time to give the tree its morning drink,' she said, and the twins followed her out into the garden. Long Ears brayed plaintively and Aunt Bee took a piece of gingerbread from her pocket. 'As if I didn't know what donkeys fancy,' she said.

'Anyone listening to you would imagine you understood what Long Ears is saying,' Kathleen said in a cheeky voice.

Aunt Bee finished giving the orange tree its drink. 'And why not, Miss? Donkeys make more sense than some people I could name.'

Long Ears swallowed the cake and turned his head to hide a smile. Aunt Bee poked him in the ribs with the spout of the watering can. 'Kindly straighten your spine and pay attention to me. I wish you to take Conor and Kathleen to the circus, where a friend of mine will make himself known when the time is ripe.'

Long Ears butted the twins with his head and they climbed up on his back. He went trotting out the gate onto the sea road, taking the direction for the village. Crowds were making for the circus and the red-haired boy was striding along in the middle of the road, a bundle of posters under one arm.

Conor was anxious to avoid trouble. He tried to steer Long Ears to one side but the donkey had often heard Aunt Bee say, 'When I drive my little blue car I refused to be pushed out of the way by a road hog.'

'Road hog,' brayed Long Ears, trotting past.

'Stupid oul' ass! Ye should stay in the bogs where ye belong,' the red-haired boy shouted, and hit the donkey with his bundle of posters. Long Ears kicked his heels up; the red-haired boy went flying in one direction and the posters in the other.

A fox who had been asleep in the ditch jumped out and went streaking along the road, followed by the donkey.

'Whoa! Steady on!' Conor tried to slow the donkey's mad gallop. 'We're not in a race,' he grumbled. Long Ears skidded to a full stop, digging in his heels. Kathleen sighed. 'Now he won't budge. Donkeys are that stubborn.'

'We'll just have to walk the rest of the way,' Conor said sourly. They jumped down and the donkey ran off, scattering people as he went.

Posters were whirling around. Kathleen picked one off the ground and read out: 'Meet the Spanish magician at the circus. He knows the past, the present and the future.' She sighed. 'I'd love to get my fortune told.'

Conor didn't believe in fortunes, but on the other hand he wouldn't mind meeting a magician, and a Spanish one at that.

At the entrance to the village, a fat, good-natured woman in a red petticoat and blue bodice was selling doughnuts. Conor rooted around in his pocket and produced some coins. 'I'll have one, please.' The

The Wily Fox

woman sprinkled a doughnut with sugar, but before she could hand it to Conor it was snatched from her hand, and the fox was racing away.

'Did you ever see the like of that for bare-faced, daylight robbery?' demanded the doughnut woman, her chin quivering with indignation. 'It's a wild animal that's after escaping from the circus.'

Conor tried to explain it was only a fox but she wouldn't listen.

'A savage animal,' she declared fiercely. 'Attacking a defenceless woman. It shouldn't be allowed.' She picked out two more doughnuts oozing with jam, sprinkled them liberally with sugar and put them in a bag. 'There you are now. One for yourself and one for the girleen who was with you just now.'

Conor thanked the woman and looked around for Kathleen. People were all making for the circus and somewhere around them a man was singing a ballad. Conor thought he recognised the voice, but couldn't be sure.

'There's that wild animal again,' the doughnut woman shouted, catching sight of the fox, which had come slinking back. The crowds began to heave and push. Conor was knocked against the fat man from the circus and saw with dismay that Kathleen was wedged between him and the thin boy with red hair. Tears were streaming down her face.

'Just what do you think you're doing?' Conor hissed.

'Why, if it isn't old Hoppity himself to the rescue.' The red-haired boy shouldered him out of the way. At the same time the fat man pushed Kathleen and she stumbled, so that the four of them went sprawling, flattening the fox that was trying to make its escape.

'Someone is biting me!' the fat man bawled.

'I'm marked for life!' screamed the red-haired boy.

'A wild animal is rampaging around!' shouted a bald man.

In the general pandemonium, the twins found themselves pushed against a wooden platform. A little black-and-white dog was holding the rim of a battered green felt hat and the Ballad Singer was singing a rousing chorus that went:

> *Oh come all ye lads and lassies and listen*
> *   to my tale*
> *Concerning a young sailor boy from the*
> *   sunny land of Spain.*
> *He longed to roam, he left his home, in a*
> *   galleon he did sail.*
> *'I'll live to fight and win a wife, and I'll*
> *   come back again.'*

Conor and Kathleen pulled themselves up on the edge of the platform and sat there, swinging their legs and munching the doughnuts, which they had managed to save. There was still another verse to go.

> *His father warned the sailor boy, 'Be sure*
> *   where'er you roam*
> *Don't lose the Sword of Destiny, the treas-*
> *   ure of your home.'*

'Oh, please don't go,' his sweetheart begged,
she cried, alas in vain.
He lived to fight, ne'er won a wife, and
never came home again.

The street had emptied. The Ballad Singer took the hat from the little black-and-white dog, brushed the brim with his sleeve and put the hat on his head.

'You didn't get any money,' Kathleen said sadly. 'They've all gone to the circus.'

''Tis small harm. I was hoping I would find you here. There's someone I want you to meet.'

They linked arms and made their way into the circus field. At the entrance to the Big Top, the red-haired boy was shouting, 'Hurry up and get your tickets here! No change given. Double price for kids.'

Standing on an orange box, the fat man was bawling loudly, 'Come inside and see my act. I chew up rocks and that's a fact.'

The Ballad Singer took a knotted handkerchief out of his pocket. He undid the knots and put down three coins. 'I want three of the best seats, please,' he said loftily.

'What about the oul' mongrel?' the red-haired boy sniggered.

'We'll feed her to the lions if she isn't too tough.' The fat man laughed and made a kick at Flash. She barked angrily and from behind the tent the fox came streaking to her aid. Teeth snapped, fur flew and the air was rent with screams, shouts and threats as the red-haired boy and the fat man fought off the furious animals. Before the dust could settle, the Ballad Singer had caught the twins by the hand and was across the field, his old coat billowing out behind him and his long skinny legs going in and out like a pair of scissors. Hard on his heels came the fat man and the red-haired boy, followed by Flash and the fox, still snapping and snarling.

5

AT THE CIRCUS

Down by the side of a yellow caravan raced the Ballad Singer, clutching Conor and Kathleen. Conor's foot was hurting and he couldn't keep up. He pulled away. 'Save Kathleen!' he called.

Behind him the red-haired boy and the fat man were closing in, shouting, 'Hiya, Hoppity. We'll do for ye now so that even yer oul' aunt won't recognise you.'

The little black-and-white dog flew at the red-haired boy, which gave Conor a chance. He doubled back on his tracks and hid behind a hayrick.

'What will I do now?' he muttered distractedly. He peeped out and saw Flash run off, wagging her tail, leaving the red-haired boy sitting on the ground with his trouser legs in tatters.

Conor waited, afraid to move. After a while, he noticed that he wasn't alone. A fox was lying beside him. He stroked the animal, holding the bushy tail. Was this the animal his aunt had been talking about the previous night? She had said that a certain fox could take a person to any place in the world he wished to be. On the spur of the moment, Conor said, 'Take me to Kathleen and the Ballad Singer.' Afterwards he was sorry he had wasted a wish on them.

He was still holding the tail when the fox leaped in the air, knocking over the rick and smothering the red-haired boy in straw. At the yellow caravan, the fox and tail parted company and Conor found himself holding a bundle of straw. Through the open window came the sound of voices and Kathleen's laugh. Crossly he climbed the wooden steps and pushed the door open. Kathleen and the Ballad Singer were ensconced at a table while a clown with a white face and a false nose was handing around tea and sandwiches. Kathleen looked up. 'So you got here at last,' she said.

'You don't care what happens to me.' A black-and-white tail thumped the ground and Conor added, rather shamefacedly, 'Flash was the only one who helped.'

Peaceably, the Ballad Singer made room on the sofa. 'Sit down and meet the person I mentioned earlier. He knows your aunt Bee of old. He spirited Kathleen and myself away from under the nose of the fat man.'

'And is telling us about his adventures,' Kathleen added, her eyes shining.

'I travelled the world with the circus,' the clown admitted modestly. He gave Conor a cup of tea and a sausage roll. 'The stories I could tell would fill a book.'

'My aunt is also a fervent traveller,' Kathleen said boastfully. 'She once went to the Friendly Islands.'

'I, too, lived in the South Seas,' the clown said, pressing a sandwich on Conor. 'What we mainly drank was coconut milk and pineapple juice.' Kathleen thought how wonderful it would be to live on a tropical island and swim around a coral reef. She sighed, and to cheer her up the clown gave her a jam tart. 'My own make,' he boasted. 'Your aunt Bee it was who first taught me to cook when she was a member of this circus.'

Kathleen wiped her fingers on a paper napkin. She looked out the window and saw the crowds making for the Big Top. A voice was calling through a megaphone: 'Hurry! Hurry! The greatest show on earth is about to begin!'

The clown jumped to his feet. 'That's my cue,' he said fussily. He ran out of the caravan, pausing to pick up a bucket of whitewash that stood at the end of the steps. Swinging the bucket, he led them across a field and into the Big Top. With a flourish, he ushered them into ringside seats and took off, still holding the bucket. The place echoed to the hum of voices and the sound of benches being filled as people found their places and settled down. A cross-faced farmer came stomping up the tent, pushing in between Kathleen and the Ballad Singer so that Flash was edged out of her seat. She trotted around the far side and sat on the aisle beside Conor. To a fanfare of trumpets, a masked figure in a red cloak swept into the ring.

'He must be the magician,' Kathleen whispered to Conor.

'I know the past, the present and the future.' The magician's voice reminded Conor of someone, but he couldn't rightly remember whom. 'I give a solemn warning to two bullies. One is fat, one has red hair. My message is: you both beware. Cheat and steal and

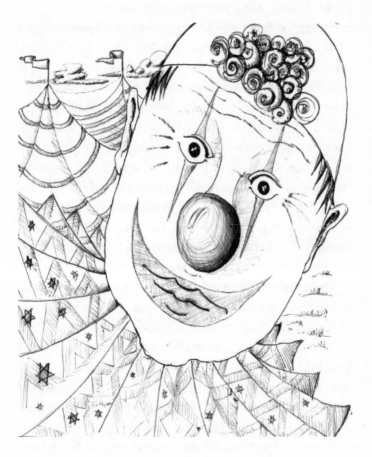

The Greatest Show on Earth

go your way. You'll wish you hadn't, you'll rue the day.'

Now it was all coming back to Conor – the sailor boy he had once met in the odd little shop . The same funny accent, the same sing-song voice.

From the back of the tent came the loud guffaws of the red-haired boy and the fat man; the laughing ceased abruptly when the magician waved his wand and the tent filled with rainbow lights. The cross-faced farmer stirred uneasily as the magician singled him out: 'You, sir, have a pig with a star on its forehead. Treat it well or else take care. You'll lose the pig before a fair. 'Ere seven days it will win a race; Dingle town the meeting place, a crock of gold the prize.'

'A pig win a race indeed,' the farmer said. ''Tis how you're making game of me. I'll not stay here to be insulted,' and the farmer jumped up and went stomping out of the tent, muttering to himself.

Once more the magician waved his wand. Singing birds rose out of the folds of his cloak and people cheered and clapped in admiration.

Once more the magician lifted his wand and pointed to where the twins sat glued to their seats. 'Conor and Kathleen are searching for a long-lost treasure,' he told the hushed tent. 'This is my message. A golden bird will take them far, into another time, and there the boy will get his dearest wish, helped by a hero old. Two diving men will rescue them, an orange tree will show the path, they'll come into a beehive hut, and find the Spanish gold.'

Conor's thoughts were wandering away to the Cave

of the Dolphins, where the sailor boy had drawn his pictures of what had happened to him, leaving a clue to the Spanish gold. Kathleen nudged him to come back to earth. The magician had gone and an elephant was parading around the ring carrying the clown, who was balancing a bucket of whitewash on his head. The elephant never forgot how the red-haired boy and the fat man had tormented him when they first joined the circus. Now, out of the corner of one small eye, he saw them creep up to where the twins were sitting.

'Now's our chance,' the red-haired boy muttered out of the side of his mouth. 'We'll nab the mongrel and keep her hostage until the oul' Ballad Singer and the twins find the Spanish gold. Then we'll trade her for the treasure.'

'And if they find nuthin', we'll drown her!' the fat man whispered. 'Have you the rope ready?'

They were getting ready to slip the noose over Flash's head when the elephant gave a mighty roar, the clown jumped in fright and the bucket of whitewash shot up in the air, coming down to drench the thieving pair. Like a couple of ghosts, they ran screeching out of the tent, while the whole place shook with laughter and people said it was the best turn of the night.

Too soon, the circus was over. People were gathering up coats and gloves, ready for home.

'Give your aunt a message from me,' the clown called from the yellow caravan. 'Tell her we'll meet some day in Granada where the fountains play. She'll remember the place. Safe journey and good luck in your search.'

'Goodbye,' chorused the twins, and the Ballad Singer promised, 'I'll see them as far as the sea road. After that, why, they're nearly home.'

They went across the fields and through the village. Long Ears was waiting and, thankfully, they climbed up on his back. Shops had their shutters up and the stalls were bare and deserted. A raggedy boy was sweeping the streets and singing softly:

I sweep the rubbish and rags so old
I weave a spell and they turn to gold

Now they had left the village far behind and were turning their faces to the sea.

'I wish I were home,' Kathleen murmured drowsily.

'I'll shorten the road,' promised the Ballad Singer, and he told them how the first leprechauns came to Ireland from the Land of the Dwarves over the sea and were well received by King Conor at his palace at Armagh. 'At that time, the rivers were running with gold and there was more gold in the mountains, so they decided to stay, and have been here with their crocks of gold ever since.'

Conor wanted to hear about the Spanish treasure.

'You know how the *Santa Maria de la Rosa* struck a rock in the Blasket Sound and went to the bed of the ocean carrying a king's ransom in gold and jewels? Ever since, it is said that the ghost of the Spanish sailor haunts these parts, looking for something he can never find.'

'And has no one ever tried to recover the gold and jewels?' Conor demanded.

'Every summer, a team of divers comes to the Blasket Sound searching for the wreck of the ship and the gold,' the Ballad Singer said. 'Maybe some day you will meet them and they will help you in your search.'

Night had fallen and the bushes that bordered the road were taking on strange shapes. At a place where the road forked – one path going by the sea, the other cutting into the mountains – the Ballad Singer left them, taking Flash with him.

'Next time you go out, be sure to take the Considering Cap with you,' he told Kathleen and, she marvelled at how he knew about it.

Along by the sea road, the night was silent and the islands remote and lonely, but the white cottage was just over the hill and a light was shining in the window. Wearily, the little donkey padded up to the door and knelt while the twins dismounted. Aunt Bee fed him carrots and gingerbread and he went trotting away to the headlands to tell the wild donkeys all his adventures.

Conor sat at the table, yawning his head off, while Kathleen helped Aunt Bee get supper and told her about the clown and what he had said.

'Well I remember Granada of the orange trees and the fountains made by the Moors when they settled in Spain hundreds of years ago,' Aunt Bee said, her voice strangely nostalgic.

Kathleen remembered the circus and how her aunt had gone travelling the world without a care. 'Where did you go? What was it like?' she asked her.

Aunt Bee seldom answered a question. She gazed into the crumbling fire and you'd know to look at her that her thoughts were miles away. 'Did you ever hear of "The Golden Road to Samarkand"?' she asked. '"Sweet to ride forth at evening from the wells, when shadows pass gigantic on the ground." I met a magician there and he gave me three wishes.'

'I know what I'd wish for,' Conor said drowsily. 'To be a champion runner.'

'I wished I could paint pictures that would come alive for special people,' Aunt Bee went on. 'I also wished for a magic mirror that would show me things as they really were. Both these wishes have come true. The third wish I still have.'

'If I met Caelte MacRonan of the Fianna, he might help,' Conor mumbled, his thoughts drifting to images of green fields, running boys and cheering crowds. 'I'd love to meet him.' His eyes were closing and he could hear Aunt Bee's voice far away.

'Ventry Strand on the far side of Mount Eagle was the great meeting place of the Fianna, and on a certain day of the year, the champions still race.'

The next thing he remembered was being in bed. Almost before his head touched the pillow he was asleep and dreaming of the Fianna running through the oak woods of old Ireland, faster than the deer.

6

Up the Airy Mountains

A horse clip-clopping along the road woke Kathleen. She peeped through the curtains and saw a cart filled with milking cans. They reminded her of the can that sat on top of the dresser and she was out of bed in less time than it takes to tell. 'I'll pick mushrooms, that's what I'll do,' she decided. 'Maybe I'll meet Long Ears and go for a ride with the wild donkeys.' She had the tingling feeling that she always got before an adventure, and was so excited that she put her jumper on inside out. The tin can was covered by the Considering Cap Aunt Bee had knitted. 'I'll wear the cap as I was advised to do,' she told herself, and ran out into the early-morning mist.

The hedgerows were laced with spiders' webs, and behind a tall hedge, voices were chattering. One louder than the rest was ordering his companion to 'Keep looking', saying 'It can't be lost'. Kathleen stood on her toes, but she wasn't tall enough to see anything. She walked along until she discovered a gap in the hedge. Two bright eyes stared back at her and then vanished. Next, a little black-and-white body wriggled through the bush and Flash was gone, racing down the sea road, followed by a shaggy goat.

Kathleen stood there, undecided as to which road to take. A robin perched on the hedge and then went zigzagging up the road towards the mountains. That decided her. She would follow the path the others had taken.

Mist was drifting down from the mountains and the path was littered with stones and potholes. Kathleen stumbled and fell into a ditch. When she picked herself up, she could see no sign of Big Tom's cabin, which was odd, because it should have been there.

'Perhaps I've gone astray,' she murmured, and indeed it looked as if she had. The field in which she now found herself was thick with mushrooms, but when she tried to pick one, it always seemed to be somewhere else. She put down her can, the better to get her bearings. Because of the mist, it was difficult to see anything and sounds were muffled, but she could distinctly make out a voice complaining, 'I'm fed up searching. I've looked every place.'

A gust of wind shook the mist free and the sun beamed down. Something shone in the grass, only it wasn't her can at all but a tiny three-legged pot. 'A real crock of gold. Fancy finding it here, of all places. Won't Conor be flabbergasted when I show him. It's as good as the Spanish treasure,' she told herself.

In the tree, the robin sang, 'Tweet, tweet.' The sound reminded Kathleen of the Spanish song Conor was always humming. She sat with her back to a boulder, hugging the crock. Far off, a dog barked and a donkey brayed. 'I wonder where Flash and Long Ears have got to.' Kathleen often spoke to herself when no one was around. She couldn't think of an answer to her question and closed her eyes. One voice louder than the rest was shouting, 'It's all your fault, you would insist on bringing it with you', and she opened her eyes again.

'It's not my fault,' a second little voice wailed. 'I only put it down for a moment and it vanished.'

Kathleen peeped around the boulder. What she saw reminded her of her aunt's favourite saying: 'When in danger or in doubt, run in circles, scream and shout.'

A crowd of little men were running around pulling on their beards in a distracted manner. Their faces were like crab apples in autumn and their eyes the colour of brown bog pools. Their coats were green, or they might have been brown, or maybe heather. They appeared and disappeared with lightning rapidity and when they stopped in their tracks, Kathleen couldn't be sure if they were there at all.

She held up the crock and spoke loudly to make herself heard against the din. 'Is this what you're searching for?' Immediately the crock was snatched out of her hand by a little man with sharp blue eyes who stood in front of her with his tummy sticking out and his eyes full of suspicion. 'Leprechauns,' said Kathleen. 'I just don't believe it.'

The little man put the crock down and sat on top of it, ready for an argument. 'And why not, may I ask? Let me tell you, young lady, that we have been around these parts for a very long time. Longer than most.' His voice was high and sharp, like the wind in the rushes.

'I know,' Kathleen agreed peaceably. 'It's just that we never see you.'

'Humph. Did they ever see a Stegosaurus or a Tyrannosaurus Rex?'

'A what?'

'Ah, that foxed you, didn't it. They're dinosaurs, that's what they are. Millions of years old. The Stegosaurus is a lizard with a miserable little brain like yours, and the Tyrannosaurus Rex is a powerful animal with a mighty brain like mine. Forty feet long and weighing twenty tons. Likes to live in the jungle, a place I never fancied, myself.'

'If people could only hear you,' Kathleen began but was interrupted.

'Arra, what difference would it make? Did you ever hear a shadow move or a sunbeam dance or the world spinning round on its axis? There's a certain way of looking at things and not always from the eyeballs out, as your aunt Bee will tell you. Anyhow, that's neither here nor there. What I want to know is why you and your brother are hounding my dog, Flash.'

'We certainly are not,' Kathleen said in high dudgeon. 'My brother once saved her from a fate worse than death.' She wasn't sure if this was true, but it sounded good.

'I met Conor in a little shop I own,' the little man said. 'He keeps a civil tongue in his head, and was neat and clean, on that occasion at least.' He stared pointedly at Kathleen's frock, which was spattered with mud, and at the Considering Cap perched rakishly on her head.

Kathleen and the Leprechauns

'I fell into a ditch coming here,' Kathleen protested, then tossed her head. 'Anyhow, it's none of your business.'

But the little man wasn't finished with his grievance. 'I swapped a most unusual mirror for Flash and don't you forget it,' he said

'Then why doesn't she stay with you? Why is she always running off? Anyone would think she belonged to the Ballad Singer.'

'Try as I will, I cannot get her to stay at home,' the little man admitted in a sad voice. 'A dog she heard of discovered a collar of gold in a rabbit burrow in a place called Glenisheen. The same collar of gold is in the National Museum in Dublin, for all to see. Now all Flash wants is to find the Spanish gold.'

The little men were whispering together. Kathleen could make out words like 'Considering Cap'.

'The crock is ours by right. Make a swap,' the little man said.

'Anyone would think I was a prisoner in the dock,' Kathleen muttered rebelliously, and at this the little man shouted, 'Silence in court!' He puffed out his cheeks and continued in an important voice: 'Our decision is this. One Considering Cap and one crock of gold in return for one tin of the best mushrooms you ever tasted, and a free pardon all round.'

Out of the corner of her eye, Kathleen thought she caught a glimpse of the Spanish sailor. She swung around, hitting her head against the tree, and for a moment stars danced. When she looked again, Flash had appeared out of nowhere and was licking her hand,

and a tin filled with pink and golden brown mush-rooms was standing at her feet. The little men had vanished.

Before Conor had gone to sleep the night before, he had been reading a story about Finn MacCool and the Wise Salmon of Asseroe. As soon as he opened his eyes, he took the book from under his pillow and continued where he had left off: 'Finn was cooking the salmon for the Druid Fineigéas. "Whoever gets the first taste will be the wisest person in the whole world," Fineigéas warned. "Be sure you do not touch the salmon." A blister rose up on the skin and without thinking, Finn pressed it down and then sucked his thumb where it stung. In that way he got the first taste of salmon and the gift of wisdom.'

A pink tongue licked Conor's nose and he put the book aside. Flash was beside him. She wriggled and pushed until he fell out of bed. When he looked around, Flash had vanished. He leaned out the window and saw her running past the orange tree.

'Mushrooms and bacon for breakfast,' sang out Kathleen from the foot of the stairs. Hurriedly Conor gave his face and hands a rub, and pulled on his trousers and jersey.

Kathleen heaped his plate with fried mushrooms. 'I was out picking these while you were still fast asleep. The adventures I had! I met a crowd of leprechauns.'

'There are no such people,' Conor mumbled, his mouth full. 'At least, *I* never met one.'

'But you *did,* when you swapped Flash for the

mirror!' Kathleen said triumphantly.

He decided to ignore her. 'Flash got me out of bed. One moment she was there, the next she was gone,' he told Aunt Bee. 'I was reading a story about Finn and the Fianna.'

Aunt Bee eyed him over the top of her reading glasses. 'You are without a doubt the most imaginative boy I have ever met, though to be quite fair, Flash was slow enough about getting you up. You should be out and about, meeting certain people.'

'What people?'

Aunt Bee was doing the crossword puzzle in the morning paper and didn't deign to answer.

Flash was sitting at the gate when Conor went out. When she saw him, she ran into the road, narrowly missing a rusty tractor that was loaded with livestock.

'Hike!' roared the driver, sticking his head out the window. He leaned out, cracking a vicious whip at Flash.

'What do you think you're doing?' demanded Conor. He recognised the driver as the same man who had stomped out of the circus at the mention of a white pig.

'You should keep your old mongrel locked up.' The driver was beside himself with temper. 'Animals are the ruination of this country. They're worse than children.'

He pulled bad-temperedly at the gears. There was a screeching sound and the tractor was off, swaying dangerously from side to side. From the crates piled high at the back came grunts and squeals of protest.

Fields ran down to the sea on one side and climbed to Mount Eagle on the other. Kathleen had come out to join Conor and they were arguing about which way to go when a rumble of wheels and a creaking of harness interrupted them, and the circus swung into view. Last in line was the yellow caravan driven by the clown. He reined in his horse and leaned down for a chat. 'I'm glad we met before I leave the district. A word in your ear: that red-haired rascal and his fat brother have left the circus. Everyone made such a mockery of them after the incident of the whitewash, they couldn't take it. I'm sure and certain they're still around and are up to no good.'

Conor's heart sank. With the tip of his toe he drew the outline of the Spanish sailor in the dust of the road and the clown nodded in sympathy. 'Don't be too worried, everything will come out all right in the end. Oh, I almost forgot. Our friend the Ballad Singer is anxious to meet the pair of you.'

Kathleen paused in chewing a blade of grass. 'Where is he now?'

'Gone up the mountains. If I were you, I'd take the next boreen into the hills. Give your aunt Bee my regards.' And the caravan was gone in a cloud of dust.

Accompanied by Flash, the twins took a road that meandered along, to finish up in a goat track. From somewhere nearby came the sound of rushing water and when they discovered a mountain stream, a grey goat was slaking its thirst, and hidden under a stone was a silver salmon. Midges were dancing in the sun. Conor longed to take off his shoes and wade upstream, but Flash and Kathleen had gone on and he was forced to follow them.

Away in the distance a fine baritone voice rang out:

I'm a roving man and I sing a song
And I don't give a thraneen about anyone.

Where the curve in the mountain straightened itself out, they caught up with the Ballad Singer striding along, his old coat billowing out behind him, the pockets stuffed with song sheets.

'Good morning, good morning, and a very good morning it is, to be sure,' he sang out. He executed a sidestep and, with the twins walking on either side and Flash leading the way, he strode along singing:

Up the airy mountains, down the rushy glen
Hide and seek and hunt around and you'll find little men.

Conor's foot was hurting him. 'I can't keep up,' he moaned. 'I'm out of breath.'

Immediately the Ballad Singer slowed down. 'I'm going so fast I'll trip myself up, though I'm advised by your aunt that exercise is good for one.'

Conor hopped along on one foot. 'Where are you going?' The Ballad Singer lit his pipe and when it was nicely drawing he said, 'I'm on my way to the Widow Crow's café in Dingle town. I've a bit of unfinished business there to conclude.' Kathleen remembered the first day they had come up the mountains with Long Ears and the storm that had followed. Today the place was different. The sun was sparkling on the blue sea far below and there was neither sign nor light of a ghostly sailing ship. There was the same heap of stones on the mountains and the Ballad Singer, straightening a tombstone, read aloud in a solemn voice, 'Here lie the last mortal remains of the Spanish sailor. He will not rest until he finds that which he seeks.'

Kathleen shivered. 'I'm scared of this place. I think it's haunted.'

'It could be you're right.' The Ballad Singer doffed his old green hat respectfully. He looked sideways at Conor. 'You know, in a way you remind me of him.'

Conor hopped on one foot. 'How so?'

'He enjoyed a bit of fun and never complained, even when things went against him, though it has to be admitted that his friends helped.'

'Who were they?' demanded the twins together.

'Well, there was the dolphin that saved him from drowning, the goat that gave him milk and a little dog like Flash here who was his constant companion. He hurt his foot in the battle of the Armada in the English Channel. After that, he walked with a limp.'

'Like me,' Conor thought. 'I'd like to meet him, even though he is only an old ghost.' He said the last bit aloud in bravado. Before the words were rightly out, he was lifted off his feet by a sudden gust of wind. He came down in a whin bush.

'You'd need to watch what you say,' the Ballad Singer cautioned, helping him up. 'Some people are easily upset, and they with grand notions of going home to a castle in Spain.'

Conor dusted his trousers and jersey off and watched while a golden eagle rose out of the bush and went soaring upwards. When the bird was out of sight, the Ballad Singer rooted around and gave Conor a golden feather. 'The eagle left this behind. Maybe some day you'll soar as high as she does.' Flash looked up at Conor with great sad eyes and began to cry.

'What's the matter with her?' Kathleen was wishing they were home and safe.

'Whenever the wind blows in a certain direction, the eagle flies back into the past. Flash is afraid the same thing will happen to Conor.'

'I don't believe such rubbish,' Conor said scornfully. What with Kathleen and her leprechauns and the Ballad Singer with his old tales, they must take him for a right sap.

The Ballad Singer stroked his beard. 'And what's so strange about going back in time? Remember, time means different things in different places.' He whistled for Flash, who was inspecting a rabbit burrow. 'Time I was on my way, and time you two were running home to your aunt. I don't doubt but she has a surprise in store for you. Conor, take care you don't let go of the eagle's feather.'

He was gone and Conor felt suddenly restless. He longed to go to Dingle town and meet the Widow Crow, and he didn't want to go home.

'Shall we follow the Ballad Singer?' he asked Kathleen, but she had had enough adventures for one day.

'I'll race you down the mountain. I'll give you a good start,' she said.

'You're bound to win,' Conor objected. All the same, he began to run. He could hear Kathleen catching up; then she easily passed him out.

'She didn't give me time,' he grumbled. To spite her, he started to saunter along. Grey clouds were gathering and the rain was blowing in from the sea. He tried to move faster but his foot hurt and the wind blew in his face.

'Time means different things in different places' – he could hear the Ballad Singer's words in his ear. He took the feather out of his pocket. 'Is this really gold? Will it bring me luck or is the Ballad Singer only joking?'

Around him the wind gathered force, lifting him off his feet and sweeping him along. When he recovered his breath he was standing at the gate of the white cottage and Kathleen was racing along the road. 'How did you get here first?' she panted. 'I passed you out.'

'He rode down the wind,' Aunt Bee sang out from the cottage door.

'I did,' Conor said delightedly. He could still feel the wind in his face, and the sensation of being carried along, faster than anything he had ever known.

'Come down to earth, you're home again,' Aunt Bee urged, and they followed her into the kitchen. She pointed to a canvas on an easel. 'Well, and how do you like my latest painting?' The picture showed a fair-haired boy racing along a strand while a man in a green cloak looked on. 'Finn MacCool is the man in green.' Aunt Bee took up her paintbrush and gave him a bronze shield and a collar of gold.

'I read about him in a book,' Conor remembered. 'He tasted the Wise Salmon of Asseroe and got the gift of wisdom.'

'Caelte MacRonan is the fair-haired boy,' Aunt Bee explained, painting in gold sandals and leather thongs criss-crossed to the knees. She studied her picture, holding her paintbrush in her mouth and wiping a speck of dirt away with her little finger. 'He could run faster than anyone else.'

'I'd love to meet him,' said Conor.

'Maybe you will, sooner than you think.'

Conor put away the paints and propped the easel against the dresser so that the picture would dry quickly, while Kathleen and Aunt Bee made a Spanish omelette and chips. For 'afters' they had roasted apples stuffed with raisins and brown sugar and covered with thick yellow cream. Across the sea, the light was fading and the islands looked lonely and remote. Aunt Bee pulled the curtains and lit the lamp. 'I just do not know where this day went,' she said. 'Already it's time for bed.'

'I'm not sleepy,' Kathleen argued. Conor pretended not to hear his aunt.

'Please remember,' she continued, 'that the race does not always go to the champion, nor the battle to the bully. The tortoise has been known to outdistance the hare and a goat can take you as far as a fox. It all depends on the company you keep and how you travel.'

She drifted out of the room, pulling the door behind her.

'I never knew such a person for speaking in riddles,' Kathleen whispered. Conor was reading a book and didn't look up.

Kathleen stared at the dresser, where Aunt Bee's picture was propped. In the firelight, the figures

Finn MacCool and Caelte MacRonan

seemed to be coming alive. 'Something very strange is happening,' she murmured, but Conor, deep in his story, paid no attention and went on reading.

7

A GOLDEN BIRD

Kathleen wasn't sure if a storm was blowing through the kitchen or if the picture was coming alive.

'What's happening?' She clutched Conor in fear.

He put down the book and they both sat listening. He found himself stroking the soft yellow fringe of the feather the Ballad Singer had given him. He remembered the circus and the magician's words: 'A golden bird will take them far, into another age, and there the boy will get his dearest wish, helped by a hero old.'

A crash shook the house and the door burst open. A whirlwind eddied around, sweeping the picture out the door.

'We'll have to recover it before it's too late,' Conor shouted, and they battled their way into the storm. Leaves, broken branches, a watering can and Aunt Bee's picture were whirling around the orange tree. A fox and a goat went flying past to hit the picture and vanish from sight.

Conor felt something move between his fingers. He looked down and saw that the feather was now attached to the body of the giant golden eagle. A gust of wind lifted Kathleen off her feet and she found herself thrown across the eagle's back.

Conor shouted, 'Be careful!'

'What did you say? I can't hear you.'

'When the wind changes, the eagle flies back into the past.'

Just at that moment, the wind veered and the eagle took off with the twins holding on for dear life. There was the sound of tearing canvas as they went in through the picture. Then everything was calm and the world was steady once more.

An amused voice said, 'That was quite a dive back in time', and a man in a green cloak lifted them off the eagle's back. They recognised him at once.

'You're Finn MacCool!' they said in unison.

'And you're Kathleen and Conor.'

'How do you know our names?' Conor still couldn't believe what had happened.

Finn smiled. 'Maybe I chewed on my thumb, or maybe I heard about you in a story our Druid told.'

'Caw, caw,' croaked the eagle, and Finn patted its ruffled feathers.

'Yes, many thanks, and the way back is over Mount Eagle,' Finn said. 'But you must hurry and ride down the wind.'

A crowd was gathered near the sand dunes, where the goat was cropping the grass and the fox stood poised against the skyline. The golden eagle wheeled sharply in the direction of the mountain and vanished from sight.

Finn tossed his cloak back and strode across the strand to where the Fianna were waiting. Conor saw with excitement that he was now dressed like a warrior, in a leather tunic and green trews. Kathleen too had changed. She was wearing a yellow cloak fastened with a gold brooch and her sandals were studded with jewels.

Beside a great fire stood an open pit where a man was roasting meat on red-hot stones. A fair-haired boy raised a goblet in greeting.

'Welcome to our visitors from another time,' he said, and all the Fianna shouted, 'A hundred thousand welcomes!'

Finn seated himself against a hillock and the feast began. They ate roast boar from bronze plates, followed by nuts and fruit and honey cakes. They drank a sparkling wine called mead that made them forget the white cottage and all they had ever known.

'I'd like to stay here forever,' Conor mused dreamily, 'if only I could learn to run.'

'Come with me, I shall teach you.' Without being told, Conor knew that the fair-haired boy was Caelte MacRonan, champion runner of the Fianna.

Along the length of the strand they ran, Caelte at Conor's elbow, timing him, pacing him, checking him, praising him, so that he felt he could run to the world's end.

'You're the best pupil I ever had, but even a champion must rest.' With his arm on Conor's shoulder, Caelte led the way back to where the Fianna were gathered. An old bearded man was plucking the strings of a harp and Kathleen was singing:

Over the ocean, across the sea
White sailing ships on a visit to me,
Dark foreign men who plied their oars
Untroubled by the wild wind's roar.

Her voice trailed away. At the entrance to the harbour a fleet of boats had appeared out of nowhere. The Fianna looked to Finn, who chewed on his thumb for guidance. When he spoke, his words held a note of doom and the twins shivered.

'Daire Donn, the King of the Eastern World, has arrived with his hordes. Before darkness falls, they will attack.' He beckoned to Caelte MacRonan. 'Go you to the High King's palace and raise the alarm.'

'Let me go with you,' Conor pleaded.

'I'll not be left behind,' Kathleen wailed.

'She's always the same,' Conor thought in despair. 'She'll spoil everything.'

But Caelte MacRonan was whistling up the grey goat and the fox. They came bounding up to his side. He swung Kathleen onto the goat's back. 'You must ride while Conor and I race. The fox will be our guide and pacemaker.'

Ever after, Conor would remember that journey through the heart of Ireland. Step by step, he kept pace with Caelte while the fox led the way. They overtook fast-moving herds of deer and bronze chariots drawn by mighty horses, flanked by Irish wolfhounds with collars of gold. At length they came to a great palace. Outside the bronze doors a company of soldiers stood guard.

'Sound the alarm! The Fianna are under attack!' Caelte shouted, and immediately horns rang out, horses whinnied, arms were unsheathed and the Tara Fianna were on their way to fight off the marauding strangers.

The battle was short but fierce, and now, across the strand, the Fianna were lighting victory bonfires and kindling torches that cast long shadows on the ground. So bright were the tapers that they dazzled the eye. It seemed that the Fianna were no more than shadows, and Finn's voice a whisper in the wind: 'Before you return to your own time you may each have a wish.'

'I wish Conor didn't limp any more,' Kathleen said softly.

Conor knew that this was the moment he had dreamt of. He wanted to make the right wish but he didn't know what it was. Someone was humming a Spanish tune. Was it Aunt Bee or the Ballad Singer or the Spanish sailor himself?

I am a Spanish sailor boy and I come from a far countr-ee

'I wish I knew what he seeks,' Conor said longingly. Finn held up his right hand. 'Look through my first and second fingers.'

Conor did as he was told. He saw a shining castle and the Spanish sailor boy buckling on a sword studded with jewels. He mounted a white horse and rode away. Conor seemed to follow the boy through the storm of battle, as the Spanish Armada fought the forces of the English queen. Then a great galleon, the *Santa Maria de la Rosa*, was limping into the Blasket Sound, sails battered and torn. Conor felt the loneliness and fear of the sailor boy as the ship keeled over, saw the boy's knuckles whiten as he gripped the sword and heard him whisper, 'This I must hide until another time. While the sword is safe, our castle stands.'

Conor was saying the words over and over. He blinked; he was back in the white cottage and Kathleen was sitting opposite him. The picture Aunt Bee had painted was on the easel, with never a scratch.

'Were we really with the Fianna?' Conor wondered.

'Can you walk without limping?' Kathleen was half-afraid to ask.

He stood up, took a few steps, whirled around and danced. 'My limp is gone! Look, I can run!'

At that moment, Aunt Bee came into the kitchen. She was humming the Spanish song and holding a box of chocolates.

'I fully realise,' she said, 'that one shouldn't eat chocolates last thing at night. All the same, this calls for a celebration.' She smiled at Conor. 'I also knew that given the proper exercise up and down Mount Eagle and along Ventry Strand, you would be cured of your limp when the time was right.'

8

Something Hidden

Aunt Bee had been working furiously all morning, first with bucket and brushes, then with polish and paints. Around her waist, a red apron was tied. Embroidered on one pocket were the words 'I Am the Boss' and on the other pocket, 'Down with Dirt'. As she worked, she sang loudly: 'Wash the dresser, scrub the floor. Polish the knocker on the door. Clean the windows, make the beds. Turn down the covers for sleepy heads.'

Conor and Kathleen were helping. They joined in with the second verse, which went:

Shake the rugs and dry the delft,
Dust the corner of the shelf,
Bake and bustle and rush and run,
A woman's work is never done.

'What about boys?' muttered Conor. 'We work just as hard.' But Aunt Bee chose to ignore him.

'Cleaning operations successfully accomplished,' she announced. 'Now for something to cool us down.'

She made a jug of lemonade and put out four

glasses. Conor carried the tray into the garden. The postman was cycling down the sea road. He had a long narrow face, drooping whiskers and a sad voice. Whenever he had a delivery to make, he stopped for a chat, and everyone liked him.

When he saw Aunt Bee and the twins, he propped the bicycle against the gate and came across the grass.

'Tormented I am this very day with that red-haired boy and the fat man,' he complained. 'Over near the bog it was and them trying to knock me off the bike and snatch the bag.' His whiskers wobbled and Kathleen was afraid he was going to burst into tears.

Aunt Bee gave him a glass of lemonade. 'Drink this up; you'll feel better,' she said.

'Once the same pair tried to hurl us over a cliff,' Kathleen said in a dramatic voice. She was prone to exaggeration. 'We had a truly fantastic escape.'

The postman sniffed. 'One of these days they'll get a horrid fright that will send them back to wherever they belong.' He handed the empty glass back to Aunt Bee, wiped his whiskers with a spotted handkerchief and took a picture postcard out of his bag. 'All the way from Egypt. I shouldn't fancy being a camel. It would give me the hump.' Chuckling to himself at his joke, he got up onto his bike and rode out the gate.

On one side of the postcard was a picture of a ruined chamber, and on the other side a message, which read: 'We have just finished excavating this underground passage of a tomb in Egypt. There should be a similar passage around Mount Eagle. We hope you are having an exciting holiday. Much love, Mum and Dad.'

While Aunt Bee gathered up the glasses and tray she told the twins, 'The Spanish sailor once hid in an underground chamber near the bog, or so it is said. Which reminds me, Big Tom is up there saving the turf. If I were you, I would join him.'

Kathleen wasn't too keen. 'We might meet that red-haired boy and his fat brother,' she said. 'Besides, it's too far to walk.'

'When I was a girl, I could walk ten miles and think nothing of it,' Aunt Bee said tartly. 'But then I never did walk. It was much more fun to run, jump, swim or fly along. However, if you insist on walking, please take note:

By the fallen beech tree, please turn right,
Soon you're in a valley, a pleasant sight,
There's a curving current, a sparkling scene,
Something hidden, yet plain to be seen.'

Kathleen loved riddles. Almost before her aunt was finished, she and Conor were running out of the wicker gate. They climbed a path behind the cottage and soon came across a fallen beech. They skirted right and went down a hill and into a valley. A stream chattered its way down a cleft in the rock, now widening into a pool, then narrowing into a rushing stream of water.

'A moving current, a sparkling scene,' Kathleen chanted. 'Something hidden yet plain to be seen.'

They knelt by the bank and peered into the water. Hidden behind a stone was a pink-and-silver salmon. Big Tom had once taught Conor how to catch a fish barehanded. 'Slide your hands around the fish. Tickle the belly and take a grip.'

The salmon wriggled, leaped in the air and landed at their feet. Conor caught the salmon by the tail and they crossed the stream, hopping from stone to stone. Away in the distance, the purple bog stretched out. Mounds of turf were dotted around like little houses.

Long Ears the donkey was chomping heather and Flash was investigating a bog hole, her bushy black-and-white tail wagging furiously. Big Tom was lighting a fire. He puffed out his cheeks and blew so hard that the turf reddened and blazed up. His face was as brown as the peat and there were white lines around his eyes from squinting against the sun.

'That's a fine class of fish you caught, Conor,' he said, holding the salmon up. 'I'll wash my hands in bog water. Then, while the kettle is boiling, Kathleen can unpack the lunch I brought with me.'

'He must have been expecting visitors,' Kathleen thought, for there were three mugs and three plates and as many knives and spoons. A homemade loaf, butter, sugar and a bottle of milk made up the picnic. Conor put the salmon down to cook on an iron pan that Big Tom produced, and watched while the skin turned golden brown and a blister rose up. He pressed the blister and sucked his thumb.

'Ouch, I burned myself,' he complained.

Big Tom grinned. 'You're like Finn MacCool and the Wise Salmon of Asseroe.'

'We met the Fianna,' Kathleen said excitedly. 'We went through Aunt Bee's picture, and Conor lost his limp.'

'You must tell me the whole story,' Big Tom said, handing around steaming mugs of tea and cuts of bread to go with the fish. When Kathleen finished, he nodded his head. 'And so it was Finn and not the Druid, Fineigéas, who got the first taste of salmon and the gift of wisdom. I'm thinking something similar has happened to our friend Conor here.'

Conor closed his eyes tightly, sucked his thumb and wished he knew what the Spanish sailor had hidden on the mountain. 'I'd like to find the underground passage Aunt Bee was talking about.' He opened his eyes. Nothing had changed. Long Ears was still munching heather and Kathleen was helping Big Tom fill the baskets with turf. Flash was chasing her tail. She stiffened, pointed her head as if listening to something and then went racing across the bog.

'She's the fastest thing on four legs,' Conor thought proudly. 'I'll follow her!' he called out. 'She might go astray!'

'I doubt but she knows every stick and stone of the place.' Big Tom was settling the pannier of turf on the grey donkey's back.

'I'm coming with you!' Kathleen yelled. In her haste, she dropped an armful of turf on Big Tom's feet and raced after Conor. He could hear her complaining loudly, 'You're going too fast!'

'I must be the fastest runner in Ireland,' he thought proudly, 'and once I was lame.'

They arrived at the edge of the bog. The turf-cutters were far behind. Bog holes had given way to rough grey boulders hewn out of rock. In front of them an earthen mound rose up.

Flash plunged through a thicket of misshapen bushes and scrub, followed by the twins. They came out at an entrance that led to an underground passage. As they arrived, the end of the little dog's tail was disappearing inside the mound.

'Come along, don't dawdle,' ordered Kathleen bossily and she plunged in after Flash.

The passage sloped downwards. All around were mysterious noises and queer rustlings.

'We're being followed,' Conor warned Kathleen.

'Don't even think of it, Conor. You know I'm scared of ghosts.'

The passage was widening into a chamber. Cautiously they felt their way around the walls.

'Pity I forgot my torch,' Conor began to say – then everything happened at once. Flash barked, Kathleen screamed and Conor was knocked to the ground. Voices were whispering loudly.

'Sit on them. Tie the oul' mongrel up.'

'Gimme some light, can't ye. It's so dark, I can't see.' A match was struck and the red-haired boy held up the stump of a candle. The fat man lit it, then bundled Flash into a sack.

'Lucky I found this in the bog. Holds more nor turf.'

'Leave our dog alone!' Conor shouted in an outraged voice. 'What do you want?'

'We folloyed ye here. You're up to somefin',' the red-haired boy said in an accusing voice.

'Bang their heads together,' advised the fat man. 'Knock them out cold. I'll smother the mongrel if she moves.'

In the flickering light the chamber looked ghostly and unreal. Walls of upright stone were decorated with strange designs of whorls and circles. A magnificent stone basin stood in one corner. Conor recalled his aunt's clue: *'Something hidden yet plain to be seen.* It surely must be here,' he thought.

Conor looked at Kathleen in the flickering light. Long ago they had worked out a series of danger signals if they were ever in a tight corner. Scratching the nose meant 'danger'. Pulling an ear meant 'listen'. Closing one eye meant 'attack'. He looked right at Kathleen and shut his right eye. She nodded, drew back and kicked the fat man on the shins with all her might. At the same moment Conor knocked the candle out of the red-haired boy's grasp. Then he dived for the stone basin. His fingers closed on a roll of paper.

In the darkness the red-haired boy and the fat man were stumbling around, uttering terrible threats. One of them caught hold of Kathleen and she screamed and went on screaming. At that moment the walls of the chamber shook. Sand and rocks were raining down on them, and a gust of wind swept across the floor.

'This whole place is caving in!' the fat man yelled, and they could hear footsteps running away.

'Wait for me, I'm comin' wid ye,' wailed the red-haired boy, his voice growing fainter and fainter.

Kathleen rooted on the ground and found matches.

'Hurry, light the candle,' Conor urged. With trembling fingers he undid the rope that bound the sack and the little black-and-white bundle wriggled free.

Another gust of wind blew out the candle. The twins

fought their way through clouds of dust and dragged themselves out of the twilight just in time. With a roar, the passage caved in, and where the entrance had been was now a heap of stones and clay. There was neither sign nor light of the red-haired boy, nor of the fat man.

'All the same, I'm glad they got away in time,' Kathleen said, dusting herself down.

'Good riddance to bad rubbish,' Conor muttered.

Flash dropped a roll of parchment at Conor's feet, her nose quivering with excitement.

'I found it in a stone basin,' Conor told Kathleen. 'I must have dropped it when the trouble started. Flash saved it.' He rubbed the little dog all over. 'You're the cleverest dog in the world.' She rolled over in an ecstasy of delight.

Conor opened the parchment. The sheet was covered with narrow, pointed writing. They couldn't make out a word.

Kathleen's teeth were chattering. 'Let's get out of here. I'm scared,' she said.

They followed Flash through the thicket and when they came out at the edge of the bog, the little black-and-white dog was gone. Conor caught Kathleen's hand and they raced along a goat track and down a boreen that led to the back of the white cottage.

'Aunt Bee, we're back!' Conor shouted as they burst into the room.

She took one look at them and threw her hands up in the air. 'Covered with dust and dirt from head to toe, and your clothes in tatters. What your parents will say, I simply do not know.'

'We were in the underground passage in the mountains; it led into a chamber. Conor found something, but we can't make out a word it says,' Kathleen said all in one breath.

Aunt Bee examined the strange old-fashioned script. 'Just as I suspected. Part of a ship's log written in old Catalan. While the pair of you are washing your hands and making yourselves tidy, I shall try to recall all the Spanish I once knew.'

But not until they had washed and changed and eaten their supper of beefsteak pie followed by jelly and cream did Aunt Bee fix her reading glasses onto the end of her nose.

They held their breath while she smoothed out the parchment and there wasn't a sound in the room while she translated the long-dead words of the captain of the ill-fated Spanish ship that had gone to the bed of the ocean in the Blasket Sound.

'This is the ninth day of September in the year of our Lord 1588, and the ship the Santa Maria de la Rosa is foundering in the Blasket Sound. Yesterday we sent a boat to the mainland offering a cask of finest wine in exchange for a cask of fresh water, but this was refused. Today we offered the ship with all the guns and a great treasure of gold plate and coins in return for help. This too was refused. As I write, a storm is blowing up and soon the ship will go to the bed of the ocean, taking all hands with her. I have persuaded the young Prince of Granada to cut adrift in a small boat and try to make for safety, if such is to be found in these dangerous times. He takes with him this, my last message and some treasure: a gold chain, the gift of his gracious majesty King Ferdinand; the Sword of Destiny, which belongs to his royal house; a blue medallion; and a little orange tree. He will plant the tree in some kind spot in memory of our ill-fated journey. The Prince will be recognised by the ring he wears, given him by the Infants of Avila, who inscribed it thus: *"No tengo mas que darte".'*

Kathleen rubbed away the tears that were rolling down her face. Conor's cheeks were pink and his eyes bright. The room was filled with the ghosts of long-dead Spanish nobles and the shadows on the wall were the ragged sails of the broken ship.

Kathleen gulped. 'What was the last bit you said?'

'*"No tengo mas que darte."* I have no more to give you. Evidently it was a betrothal ring. Long ago, children were promised in marriage, especially children of noble birth. Such was the custom.'

'The Princess waited and he never came back,' Kathleen said sadly.

'He must, he will,' Conor vowed. 'If only we knew where he hid his treasures.'

Aunt Bee pulled the curtain aside and gazed out into the night. 'Did either of you notice,' she asked suddenly, in a matter-of-fact voice, 'how the orange tree is improving, growing tall and straight and strong? Soon it will be possible from the top to see right over the peninsula, and when that happens, who knows, the mystery may be solved.'

The Escape of the Prince of Granada

9

The Dingle Races

On the morning of the Dingle Races, Conor and Kathleen were up and dressed as soon as the sun rose over Mount Eagle, and in no time at all they had finished breakfast and were helping Aunt Bee to sweep the floor and wash the dishes. Conor found a silver coin with a hole in the middle and Kathleen discovered a blue silk ribbon under a cushion; she tied the ribbon in a bow in her hair.

Aunt Bee fixed her hat, which had a long green feather, in front of the mirror Conor had given her as a birthday present. When she moved her head, the feather swayed back and forth. 'Indeed, I am a very stylish woman,' she told her reflection. 'I have a certain *je ne sais quoi*. Something tells me I should take an umbrella on this outing.'

Conor was standing at the front door. 'I don't know why you need an umbrella. The sun is splitting the rocks.'

'In Dingle the weather is as unpredictable as a pig running a race,' Aunt Bee said airily. She put the mirror into a white shopping bag, picked up her umbrella from the stand and went out the door. She rolled back the hood of her little blue car and waved the twins into the back. 'I wish to leave room in front, so that any stray traveller who decides to join us may do so without undue difficulty.' She settled herself comfortably in the driving seat and turned the ignition key. 'Remind me,' she said as the car moved off, 'to buy gingerbread in Dingle town for Long Ears.'

'I can't help feeling we're wasting the day,' Conor said glumly. 'We should be up the mountains or over on the Blaskets, searching for clues for the Spanish treasure.'

'The treasure has been lying wherever it is for over four hundred years,' Aunt Bee said over her shoulder. 'Another day will not make a difference. Besides, it is important that we attend the races. Who knows what we may pick up.'

As they drove along, the twins played a game of counting objects they passed that began with the letter 'T', but the green feather was blocking Kathleen's view.

'I can't see properly on this side,' she complained. 'Would you please removed your hat, Aunt Bee, or at least the feather?'

'I find it necessary to keep my hat firmly anchored to my head,' Aunt Bee said sternly, 'besides which, the feather indicates which way the wind is blowing. These considerations should outweigh any temporary inconvenience you may be caused.'

They climbed a hill and Aunt Bee sounded her horn as an indication that she was about to pass a tractor containing a litter of pigs. As she did so, a white pig gave a flying leap and landed in the passenger seat.

Conor was mesmerised. He couldn't take his eyes off the pig. Aunt Bee drove steadily on as though nothing unusual had happened.

'That's the farmer we met at the circus,' Kathleen said, craning her head to look back. 'The magician told him that the pig with a star on its forehead would win the Dingle races. The farmer is wild with temper. The pig belongs to him, you know.'

'As a matter of interest, the pig is his own master and is quite entitled to hitch a lift,' Aunt Bee said briskly. 'I need hardly add that the farmer is a very ill-natured person at the best of times.'

Conor remembered a dream he had had the previous night. 'I was walking along with the Spanish sailor and the leprechaun passed us. He was riding that selfsame pig.'

'He's welcome,' Kathleen sniffed. Pigs were not her favourite animals.

'You might remember that quite a number of people would like to be on the pig's back,' Aunt Bee said coldly. 'They persist in trying to make a silk purse out of a sow's ear. No doubt the pig is as little anxious to carry you as you are to ride.'

The pig turned, winked at Kathleen, and then began to snore in a pointed manner.

They drove along by the river over a humpback bridge, and Dingle harbour swam into view. Beyond the harbour the town stretched out, a warren of narrow, winding streets, high, red-bricked chimney pots and painted spires.

Aunt Bee parked her car beside the sea wall and the pig jumped out and trotted away. She tapped the car with her umbrella and the hood sprang back into place. 'Precautions, lest the rain should come. Come along, don't dawdle,' she ordered as they followed her into the town.

A handsome gypsy girl with gold earrings and scarlet ribbons in her hair caught Kathleen's arm. 'Cross my palm with silver. I see great luck coming your way.'

'Cross the gypsy's palm with that silver coin you found,' Kathleen begged Conor.

He didn't believe in fortunes, yet he did as Kathleen asked.

'You are both in the middle of a great adventure,' the gypsy said, peering at Kathleen's hand. 'In the end you will get a valuable gift from a noble lord, or maybe a prince from across the sea. The end of your search will be found at the top of an orange tree, and you will all live happily ever after.' She grabbed hold of Conor's hand. 'A white pig will bring you a power of luck. You should enter for the Dingle Races. When the last toffee apple is sold, the tin will turn to gold.'

Kathleen was very impressed. 'Did you hear that bit about a valuable gift and a prince and the orange tree?'

Conor sniffed. 'I did and a load of rubbish about tin turning to gold. Honestly, you'd believe anything you were told.'

A thin, raggedy, fair-haired boy held out a tray of toffee apples. 'Buy my sweet juicy apples,' he called in a high, clear voice.

'Only for that old gypsy, I could have bought some with my silver coin,' Conor muttered. 'Where's Aunt Bee got to?'

'Over there at the gingerbread stall,' Kathleen said, peering about her. The feather in Aunt Bee's hat was like a beacon, beckoning them on. She was filling her white bag with gingerbread for Long Ears and she paused to introduce the twins.

'Permit me to introduce my niece, Kathleen, and her brother, Conor.'

'The little girl is like you only your hair is red and hers is yellow and your eyes are green and hers are blue. The boy isn't like you at all, at all,' said the stall-keeper, handing them each a cake.

'Gingerbread is good but not filling,' the woman continued. 'You should visit the Widow Crow's café. She makes good strong tea and her ham sandwiches are a treat.'

Aunt Bee nodded. 'Just what I was thinking myself. I shouldn't be surprised if she has a message for someone I know.'

The twins followed her into a cobbled lane where an old-fashioned shop with diamond-shaped windows stood. A sign swinging in the wind said:

Hop in and Have a Peck at the Widow Crow's Café

They found themselves in a room with yellow walls and a moss-green carpet. One wall was decorated with china birds in flight. A tiny woman was setting a table beside the window. She put a clawlike hand on Conor's head and chirruped: 'I have a message for the young lad here. He is to be sure and enter for the Dingle Races.'

Kathleen pulled her aunt's arm in excitement. 'She's the second person today who told him that selfsame thing. The first was a gypsy.'

'It would be as well for him to eat something first,' Aunt Bee said as the Widow Crow came back with a large teapot and a plate of sandwiches. 'One cannot expect to win a race on an empty stomach.'

When they had finished eating, Aunt Bee took a bundle of postcards out of her bag. 'It's time the pair of you were off to the races. Come back before the rain does. Meanwhile I shall remain here and occupy myself by writing to some very important people I know.'

'Would you mind telling us who they are?' Kathleen couldn't bear not to know what was happening.

'My friends in the circus, as well as a couple of deep-sea divers in London, friends of mine. It is about time they paid a visit to the peninsula. Something tells me they may be needed soon.'

Beside the racecourse, a banner was strung across the road with words written on it in gold:

Final Event: Grand Crock of Gold Race.
Open to One and All. Any Animal You Fancy.

'We forgot to get money from Aunt Bee to enter the racecourse,' Conor said in a temper. 'She should have remembered.'

'We could climb over the wall,' Kathleen suggested.

Conor bent down. 'Get up on my back and pull yourself up, then give me a hand.'

They sat on the wall, swinging their legs and watching the crowds below. They saw gypsies selling lace and telling fortunes, the cross farmer, a dark-haired boy with a limp who could have been the Spanish sailor, and the white pig with a star on its forehead, followed by a shaggy black-and-white dog.

'There's Flash!' Conor shouted, wobbling danger-ously.

'And the leprechaun,' yelled Kathleen, pointing to where a small figure in green was darting between the crowds.

Conor craned his head, lost his balance and fell off the wall, fortunately coming down on the inside. He picked himself up and shouted to Kathleen. 'Jump down! I'm following Flash.' He didn't wait to see Kathleen jump but was off in hot pursuit. At the top of the field the crowds had thinned and a group of riders, their mounts saddled and ready, were clustered around a table. A three-legged pot glinted in the sun, and a familiar voice was shouting, 'Amn't I after telling ye, it's gold and filled to the brim with money.'

'Yerra, 'tis only an old tin can,' a red-faced farmer shouted angrily. Conor recognised him as the owner of the white pig.

A jockey in a striped jersey shook his fist. 'This whole race is a fraud. You should be reported.'

With that, the crowd parted and Conor came face to face with the fat man. He waved the crock in Conor's face, bawling loudly, 'I'm in charge here and I tell you it's gold!'

Animals and riders had melted away. Only a pigtailed girl on a pony remained. A wicked black horse ridden by the red-haired boy came thundering up the field.

'I'm not getting mixed up with the likes of them,' Conor muttered in a panic. He backed out of the way of the black horse, tripped and found himself on the white pig's back. Somehow the pig appeared to have grown larger and was sporting Kathleen's green hair ribbon done up as a rosette.

An elegant steward wearing a tall hat, striped grey trousers and a rose in his buttonhole was appealing to everyone to clear the course. 'Will you please get out of the way of the riders, or you'll be maimed, or killed stone dead, or worse.'

'I never thought I'd see the day when a pig would be allowed in a race. I must say, it is cool,' the girl with the pony said in an amused voice. She kicked her mount and the pony trotted over to where the black horse was prancing around.

Angrily, the steward chased a couple of boys away, the flag dropped and the race was on.

Right from the start, the black horse was out in front, though the pony was making good ground. Away down the field the white pig was mincing along.

'Will you get a move on,' Conor hissed frantically in the pig's ear. All around, people were laughing and calling out rude remarks.

'Stick it out and you'll win by a pig's head,' the jockey shouted, dancing with glee.

'Have a care or you'll wear out his trotters.' The farmer was purple-faced. 'That pig is mine and I'll hold you responsible.'

Conor tried to dismount. Somehow, he was wedged on the pig's back and couldn't move.

'Giddy up, giddy up,' Kathleen shouted, getting all mixed up. On one side of her was Flash with her paws up on the fence; on the other was a little man in green with a bald head, looking remarkably like the little man in the shop who had swapped the mirror. Flash barked and the little man gave a piercing whistle. At that, the pig leaped in the air and was gone, streaking along in the wake of the pony. Now pig, pony and horse were neck and neck, hooves and trotters pounding the turf while the roar of the crowd reached a crescendo. As they came in sight of the winning post, the white pig put on an extra spurt and came home the winner by a pig's head.

Kathleen darted across the field, dodging the crowds throwing their hats in the air. By the time she reached Conor, he had collected the prize and the pig was nowhere in sight.

'You are a champion and no mistake,' she said, hugging her brother while people streaming past clapped him on the back.

'Yerra, you're a great boy yourself. Not many would win a race and he riding the likes of a pig.'

In the crush the twins were swept over the race-course and out the gate. Here they stopped to examine the crock, which was made of tin. A few coins rattled around the bottom.

The Racing Pig

'You were cheated,' Kathleen said indignantly.

'I don't mind a bit.' It was the first prize Conor had ever won and he was walking on air.

'What will you do with the money?' Kathleen said.

'I'll buy you a present.' From a bookstall he picked out a book about ancient Egypt for Kathleen, and chose a silk scarf for Aunt Bee from another stall. He bought a string of sausages for Flash, who took them gratefully and ran off. A pink snout nudged Conor over to where the thin raggedy boy was standing and Conor spent the last of his money on a toffee apple for the pig.

'You bought something for everybody,' Kathleen said proudly. 'A book for me, a scarf for Aunt Bee, sausages for Flash and a toffee apple for the white pig. You've nothing left for yourself.'

Conor felt the crock grow heavy and Kathleen remembered what the gypsy had said: 'When the last toffee apple is sold, the tin will turn to gold.'

'Do you think it is gold?' she rubbed the rim of the crock with her finger. She could hardly believe her eyes. 'It *is* gold, Conor.'

Conor wondered who was responsible – Flash, the white pig, the little man he had first met in the shop, the gypsy or the raggedy boy. He looked around. They had all gone and the street was grey and empty. A sharp wind blew up from the harbour and dark clouds scudded across the sky.

'Aunt Bee warned us to be back before the rain came,' Kathleen remembered, and they ran up a lane in search of the Widow Crow's café.

Aunt Bee was standing outside the diamond-shaped

windows. As they came up, she tucked the birthday mirror into the shopping bag, which also held her purse and the gingerbread for Long Ears.

'I did so enjoy watching the race,' she told them in a pleased voice. 'The mirror was ever so clear.' She tied the scarf Conor had given her under her chin, so that the ends stuck out like propellers on a plane. Then she slipped her shopping bag over one arm and opened the umbrella.

'Link me now,' she ordered. 'That's right. Tighten your grip and when I count to three, jump as high as you can.' A gust of wind caught the umbrella, which went sailing over the church spires and rooftops of the town. They drifted down to earth by the harbour where the little blue car, with the hood securely fastened, was parked. They climbed in and took the road around by Ventry harbour back to the white cottage by the sea.

10

The Third Wish

Long Ears the donkey came trotting down the sea road and jumped over the garden wall of the white cottage. He went up to the kitchen window, which was open, and put in his head. Kathleen was drawing a funny bearded face on her eggshell, topped with a Considering Cap, while Aunt Bee was reading aloud a postcard which had arrived that morning: '"Greetings from the circus. We are playing in Dublin to packed houses. Any sign of the red-haired boy or the fat man? Are they still in your part of the world? Keep an eagle eye out for them, for they are up to no good, and do beware of things that go bump in the night. We hope that the orange tree has grown even taller. Good luck in your search. Your sincere friend, the Clown."'

Conor was dreaming about the day he spent with the circus. 'Shall I ever see them again?' he wondered.

'Conor, wake up,' Aunt Bee ordered briskly. 'This is our last day here and you should be out and about in the fresh air. As you are well aware, tomorrow we pack our bags and take the road for home. Kathleen, do give up playing with your eggshell.'

Long Ears didn't wait to hear any more. He wandered away, moodily swishing his tail. This was a morning of sudden shocks. First there was what he had seen from the headlands in the early morning: strange figures dressed in rubber suits and goggles sailing for the island. And now Aunt Bee's bombshell. Soon the halcyon days of carrots and gingerbread, wild gallops up the mountains or down to the village – all these would be things of the past. They could hear him braying in the kitchen and Kathleen looked at her aunt with doleful eyes.

'What will happen to Long Ears when we are gone?' Kathleen asked.

'I understand Big Tom intends to buy a donkey cart. They'll have great times trotting to the bog and bringing home seaweed from Coumeenole strand.' She rose to her feet and went to the window, shading her eyes as she looked out. 'If only the clown could see the height of the orange tree, he wouldn't believe his eyes. There's a star-shaped cloud over the island, a sure sign of adventure. You could spend your last morning at Coumeenole.'

'Will you paint a picture?' Conor asked hopefully. 'You could do one of the Spanish ship. Maybe a hurricane would blow up and we could go through the picture and find the treasure.'

Aunt Bee shook her head. 'My painting holidays are finished. When I have cleared the breakfast table and put the house in order I shall occupy myself by making sandwiches and coffee for any visitors who may drop in.' She wore a secretive smile and Conor wanted to ask who the visitors might be but was distracted by the braying of the donkey.

'You'd best be off. Long Ears can't wait much longer,' Aunt Bee warned.

Kathleen put her spoon through the eggshell and followed Conor out into the garden. They climbed onto the donkey's back and he kicked up his heels and went out the gate. They passed hedges of scarlet and gold and fields covered with bog cotton. Wisps of cloud floated overhead and the sun shone warmly. And yet the field mice and the badgers and the fox in his lair, as well as the wild geese on the wing, knew that the last of summer had come. At the clifftop, the donkey stood waiting patiently while the twins jumped down.

'I'll miss you, Long Ears,' Kathleen said in a muffled voice, her face pressed against the donkey's shaggy coat. He nudged her affectionately and then ran off to join his wild companions on the headlands.

Kathleen followed Conor down the winding path that led to the cove. She felt she could almost touch the Blasket Islands, they looked so near. Cattle were drinking at a spring that toppled over the cliff and Flash was barking at a reckless cow that wished to go swimming. Further along the beach, Big Tom was collecting seaweed to fertilise his patch of land on the mountains.

'Where's the Ballad Singer?' Conor shouted.

Big Tom straightened up. 'Out with the divers. Ever since daybreak, they're scouring the waters for the Spanish ship. I wouldn't doubt but they'll lift her today.' He pointed southwards to where a boat lay motionless on the water.

Kathleen came up, panting and out of breath. 'I know all about the divers. Aunt Bee invited them. She sent them a postcard on the day of the Dingle Races.'

'So well you didn't tell me.' Conor pulled a face and walked away, kicking stones. Flash left the cow at the water's edge and followed him.

Kathleen sighed. 'Now he's sulking. Aunt Bee said he got out of the wrong side of the bed.'

'It happens to the best of us,' Big Tom said. 'Leave him alone and he'll get over it. Here, help me fill up with seaweed.'

When the sack was full, the big fisherman hoisted it over his shoulder and was gone, driving the cows before him up the cliff.

Kathleen took off her shoes and hopped along by the edge of the sea. Waves were breaking on the sand and the cold sea foam swirled around her ankles.

A seagull skimming along on the crest of the waves watched her with beady eyes, then flew around by the headlands.

Somewhere around, a dog was barking. Kathleen waded in and out amongst the rocks. She found Conor stretched on a flat rock that jutted into the sea. Flash was jumping up and down, barking at seabirds.

Kathleen pulled herself up beside Conor. 'I forgot to tell you about the divers. Honest I did. Anyhow, what difference would it have made?'

Conor gazed wistfully out at the Great Blasket Island. 'I could have gone with them. I should have been there when the treasure was found. I tried so hard.'

'Maybe they won't find anything,' Kathleen said sleepily. Her eyes felt heavy and the air was full of the kind of closeness that comes before a storm. She was sorry for Conor, remembering the day they had spent on the island and how they had found the Cave of the Dolphins and the message on the wall.

She pressed her fingertips against her eyelids and it was dark like the underground passage on the mountains. 'Did the sailor boy ever go back to the island?' she wondered. 'Where did he hide his treasures? He took so many things with him when he left the ship.'

She was asleep and dreaming she was flying over the sea on the back of the golden eagle. Then the dream changed and she was standing on the Great Blasket Island holding up Aunt Bee's mirror. 'Beware of the sea!' screamed the mirror. Only it wasn't the mirror at all but the cry of a seagull. She awoke with a start. Gulls were screaming overhead and Flash was whimpering miserably. She shook Conor awake. 'The tide is in and we're trapped,' Kathleen said.

He jumped up in alarm. 'What happened?' he said.

Below them the sea was green and treacherous, churning angrily, sending showers of spray over the rocks. Storm clouds covered the islands.

'I'll go for help,' Conor said in a distracted voice.

'You can't. You'll be drowned.'

Flash crept to the edge of the rock and stood there trembling. Then she flattened her ears and before they could stop her, she had leaped into the raging sea. She was making for the Great Blasket Island, battling against the terrible seas, now rising with the waves,

Flash Leaps into the Stormy Sea

now sucked down in the monstrous hollows.

'She'll drown,' Conor moaned.

Kathleen was crying, 'Come back, Flash!' but her voice was lost in the roar of the sea.

Far out, a gigantic wave was gathering force, rolling towards them. Then, like a giant waterfall breaking, spray was pouring over the rocks, sucking them down.

'I'm drowning,' was Kathleen's last thought as she seemed to go down into a green and frightening kingdom. She remembered no more until she opened her eyes to a stormy sky. She was lying wrapped in a rug on a grassy patch on the headlands and the world was steady once more.

'Drink this up,' urged the voiced of the Ballad Singer, and he held out the top of a flask.

She swallowed something hot and stinging and coughed.

'Where's Conor?' she gasped when she got her breath back, and then saw with relief that he was sitting on the step of a station wagon, wearing a coat much too big for him. Beside him sat a bearded man and there was another man gathering up diving gear.

The Ballad Singer carried Kathleen over and introduced his companions. 'This bearded scoundrel is Stephen,' he chuckled, 'and this is his co-diver, Don.'

'Your aunt wrote and told us about your adventures,' Stephen said, smiling.

'They were telling me about the wreck.' Conor was wide-eyed with excitement.

Don threw the last of the diving gear into the back of the wagon. 'Time to get them back to the cottage,' he advised Stephen. 'I'll go down to the sea to the boat.' The Ballad Singer whistled for Flash and she came out from under the wagon, still shaking herself dry. She followed the Ballad Singer and Don down to the slip, while Stephen bundled the twins into the wagon and drove off.

'How did you find us?' Kathleen demanded. She could see Stephen's brown smiling eyes in the driving mirror.

'We were near the bed of the ocean when the dolphin alerted us. We surfaced and saw your dog. She was almost exhausted. We took her into the dinghy and got to you just in time.'

Conor whistled. 'We had a narrow escape.'

The door of the white cottage was open and Aunt Bee was waiting, brushing tears from her face. Stephen bundled the twins into the kitchen. 'They're safe and sound, Bee, no harm done.'

It was only when they were warm and dried and sitting beside the fire eating soup and sandwiches that she finally relaxed.

'I was never so worried in all my life. I knew something dreadful was happening. Tell me all,' Aunt Bee said.

'Flash raised the alarm when we fell into the sea, and the divers rescued us,' Kathleen said. 'Flash is helping us search for the Spanish treasure. A dog she once heard tell of found a collar of gold down a rabbit burrow.'

The big bearded man lit his pipe and sat back. In a way he reminded them of Big Tom – the same sharp eyes, and a face tanned by wind and sea. 'Early this morning,' he said, 'we brought up guns and a cannon. My guess is that the gold was swept away when the ship broke up.'

Conor frowned. 'There must be treasure somewhere around. Long ago, the Spanish sailor hid all he carried. We found a message from the captain of the *Santa Maria de la Rosa* hidden in an underground passage.'

'He wrote that the young Prince of Granada took with him a gold chain, a sword, a medallion and the orange tree that grows in the garden,' Aunt Bee said.

'And don't forget the ring he got from the Princess of Avila,' Kathleen put in.

Stephen didn't reply. He filled his pipe, pulled hard, and a long ribbon of smoke made an oval shape.

'Beehive hut,' Kathleen said excitedly. 'Remember what the magician said.'

'Two diving men will rescue them. An orange tree will show the path, they'll come into a beehive hut and find the Spanish gold,' Conor recited.

Aunt Bee gazed into the hearth. 'Beehive hut,' she murmured. 'There must be dozens of them around the peninsula. Old stone buildings, hundreds of years old. Now only the animals shelter there.'

Stephen knocked his pipe on the hearth and put it away. 'When we first got the idea of diving in the Blasket Sound, we went to the records office in London. There we examined a chart of the islands dating back to the time of the Spanish Armada. If my memory serves me right, there was a beehive hut on the Great Blasket Island used by smugglers.

Wind screamed around the cottage, rattling the windows and doors. 'If the wind doesn't change, chances are the islands will be cut off for weeks,' Stephen warned.

Conor looked woebegone and Stephen patted his shoulders. 'Don't worry,' he said, 'we'll be back in the autumn. If we discover the beehive hut we'll send you word.'

'I want to discover it myself,' Conor thought, but he didn't say this aloud. Instead he asked in a small, disappointed voice, 'If you find the treasure, will you keep it?'

The diver looked across at Aunt Bee. He seemed to be waiting for her to say something.

'What belongs to the divers is the wreck, complete with guns and cannon. No one can take that from them. What belongs to the Spanish prince is the Sword of Destiny, the golden chain, the medallion and the ring. No one dares take them away. Conor and Kathleen were given a crock of gold, and the orange tree is mine.' Her voice was solemn, as if she wanted someone outside the four in the room to take heed.

Night had fallen and Stephen had gone, driving back up the mountains to Big Tom's cabin. The twins were drinking cocoa and Aunt Bee was reading a book.

'All the same, it's a pity we didn't meet the divers before,' Conor remarked wistfully. 'I'm sure they would have been a massive help.'

His mind was still whirling with the stories Stephen had told them – how he had ridden on the back of a shark and how Don had escaped from a giant jellyfish called a Portuguese man-of-war that lived at the bottom of the ocean.

'At least we know where to look,' Kathleen consoled him. 'If only we could get over to the island just once more.'

Outside, the wind was changing, and far away a horn gave warning of a ship in distress. Conor thought about the first time he had met the Spanish sailor in that strange little shop. It all seemed so long ago. 'Show us your magic mirror,' he begged his aunt. 'Maybe we'll see the Spanish sailor again.'

She put down her book and went into the bedroom to fetch the mirror. They couldn't be sure if the glass was misted or if what they actually saw was the inside of a beehive hut.

Conor pushed the mirror aside. 'We might as well give up. We're beaten.'

'We'll come back next summer and have another try,' Kathleen said, trying hard to cheer Conor up. She began to count how long – hours into days into weeks into months. There were so many, she couldn't keep track.

Aunt Bee put an arm around each of them. She might have been anyone's aunt, except the twins knew full well that strange things had a habit of happening when she was around, and that she was distinctly odd and seldom if ever explained what she meant.

'You may recall my telling you that when I was a girl, I was given three wishes.'

'You wished you could paint a picture that would come alive,' Kathleen began.

'And that you would own a mirror that would show you things as they really are,' Conor put in. He wanted some credit for the mirror.

'Quite right. As you are both aware, two wishes have come true: the golden mirror and the picture of Finn and the Fianna. Do not forget that I still have one wish left. Now, I think the time has come at last to test the magician's words.' She stood up, and her shadow, which reached the ceiling, looked immensely tall and commanding. 'I wish that before we leave this place, Conor and Kathleen will find what they are seeking and that the Spanish sailor will be able to go home at last.'

The twins held their breath while the tick-tock of the clock on the mantelpiece grew louder and the wind outside dropped away. A flame shot up the chimney, lighting up a painting that hung over the mantelpiece. A sailor boy held up a golden sword while two shadowy figures looked on. Then the fire crackled and sank, the shadows changed and the painting was a thorn tree on a hillside.

'Your wishes didn't work,' Conor whispered.

'Wishes come true when you least expect them,' Aunt Bee said softly, 'and now it's time for bed.'

11

THE END OF THE SEARCH

Outside, the storm had died away and the garden was full of broken lights and strange long shadows. One had long ears, another had horns, and some had beards and pointed caps. They stayed very still while two figures crept around by the side of the cottage. A window was pushed open and someone climbed in.

Through his dreams, Conor heard a muffled thud which seemed to come from a long way off. He rubbed his eyes and sat up. He was still half-asleep. He got out of bed, pulled on his trousers and jersey, then crept outside, carrying his shoes. Kathleen was standing outside the kitchen door. She was fully dressed and was even wearing a tam-o'-shanter. The door was half-open and the room was lit by the flickering coals in the fire. The red-haired boy was reaching up to the dresser.

In an instant Conor was across the room. 'You rotten thief,' he hissed. 'Just what do you think you're up to?'

'Leave me alone.' The red-haired boy waved the crock of gold in the air. 'This is ours by right. You cheated, riding your oul' pig at the races.' He brought down the crock with all his force on Conor's head, but it only bounced harmlessly and went rolling across the floor.

Before Conor could stop him, the red-haired boy was gone through the window. In the garden, a hoarse voice was demanding, 'Well, did you get it?'

Kathleen picked up the crock. 'It's only rubber. Maybe it's just as well, or it would have brained Conor.' He had followed the red-haired boy into the garden and she went to see what was going on.

For a breathless moment, not a leaf stirred. Then everything happened at once. From the top of the orange tree came a long-drawn-out whistle. Conor had heard the same signal at the Dingle Races. As if in answer, a grey-horned animal leaped out of the darkness and the red-haired boy was tossed in the air.

High above, the moon sailed out from behind a cloud, lighting up the sea road, where two figures were running for their lives. Their terrified voices wafted back:

'A mad goat nearly killed me.'

'I was attacked by a vicious donkey.'

'There were dozens of little men who kicked and pinched me.'

'The whole country is haunted.'

'I'm goin' back to Dublin and you won't get me back here in a hurry.'

They were gone and the place was silent once more. Conor looked up at the orange tree. He could have sworn that he saw a bearded face wearing a Considering Cap staring down. He swung out of a branch and pulled Kathleen up. They climbed to the top. No one was there.

From where they were seated on the topmost branch, they could see right over the peninsula. On one side, Mount Eagle rose up, and in the opposite direction was the Blasket Sound. The moon had thrown a silver path across the dark water and a boat lay motionless in the shadow of the island.

'Is it the Spanish ship?' Kathleen whispered.

'I don't know,' Conor whispered back.

Conor pointed to where a burst of light lit up the sky. 'Someone is sending up flares at the pier. We had better find out who it is.'

Quickly they scrambled down the tree. Long Ears was waiting and they lowered themselves onto his back. He gave a great leap and was out the gate in an instant and thundering along the sea road. Parked at the top of the pier was the divers' station wagon. Below, a motorboat was pulling away.

'Wait for us!' Conor shouted frantically. His voice was drowned by the noise of the engine. Long Ears threw back his head and the sound of harsh braying rent the night. In the boat, Flash was barking loudly. The boat was turning.

'They're coming back!' Conor shouted.

Kathleen hugged the little donkey. 'You saved the night, Long Ears!'

She followed Conor down the flight of winding steps. As they reached the water's edge, the boat moved into the landing slip. They could make out the two divers as well as the Ballad Singer. Big Tom was at the wheel.

'What happened?' Conor called out.

The Ballad Singer swung them down and into the boat. 'There's a ship in distress. We were having a game of cards at Big Tom's house when we heard the signal. We got down as fast as we could.'

'We sent up flares to alert the coastguard,' Stephen said. 'The lifeboats should be out by now.'

Big Tom let out the throttle and the boat tore across the Sound. Before them, the Great Blasket was looming up. Fishing boats were circling around and the trawler was tilted at an awkward angle.

'The storm blew her off-course,' a lifeguard shouted.

Big Tom made a megaphone of his hands and shouted, 'Who is she?'

'A Spanish fishing trawler,' came the reply.

They were rounding the island and coming into the landing place. As soon as the boat stopped, Flash leaped onto the pier. The Ballad Singer helped the twins up. 'You'll be fine here,' he said, jumping back into the boat.

'We're going to the trawler to lend a hand,' Big Tom called up from the wheel. 'We'll pick you up later.'

Conor sat on an upturned lobster pot and Kathleen perched beside him. She drummed her heels against the pot and said, 'We got to the island after all.'

'And what now?' Conor thought. The orange tree had grown in Aunt Bee's garden, but where was the Sword of Destiny and the other treasures the captain had written about in the ship's log?

Kathleen stared across the dark water. 'Did the sailor ever reach this island?'

'He must have. Remember the painting in the Cave of the Dolphins,' Conor reminded her.

'We should search for the beehive hut,' Kathleen said, and shivered. The place was gripped by an eerie silence. Dark shadows were everywhere. Flash too was behaving curiously, rolling herself up in a ball, then sniffing around. She stiffened and was gone, running up a winding path that led to the cliffs. She kept looking back to see if the twins were following.

She led them around a hill and across a field. Overhead, the moon had disappeared and the stars were only pinpricks of light in the dark. A grey stone building rose up before them.

Kathleen clutched Conor's arm. 'A beehive hut,' she said.

He nodded. 'Remember the magician in the circus. He said that "Two diving men will rescue them. An orange tree will show the path. They'll come to the beehive hut".'

'And find the Spanish gold,' Kathleen finished breathlessly. Flash looked back, her eyes glittering. Then she had gone, through the opening.

Resolutely, the twins followed her in. At that moment, the moon cut loose from a cloud, filling the hut with light. Underfoot, the clay was choked with nettles and weeds. Stones were scattered all around.

Flash whimpered, pawing a stone that had strange markings of whorls and lines. They had seen a similar stone in the underground passage near the bog.

'She wants us to move the stone,' Conor said. They tried.

'Too heavy,' panted Kathleen.

Conor remembered a picture his father had once shown him. It depicted burial stones in an Egyptian chamber. He examined the stone and found the same deep groove on either side. 'Catch hold this side,' he told Kathleen. 'I'll do the same at the other side and when I give the word, push.'

The stone slowly moved, tilting to one side. Underneath, the clay was soft. Flash began to dig furiously. Her nose was covered with dirt and her paws moved so fast that clay flew in all directions. She was whimpering, worrying something, then she jumped out of the hole and stood looking at them, tail wagging for all she was worth.

'I'll see what it is.' Conor knelt by the side of the hole. 'There's something here. Give me a hand.'

Between them, they lifted out a wooden box. As they put it on the floor, the lock fell apart. They looked at each other, afraid to speak. Then, slowly, Conor raised the lid. Lying on a bed of faded velvet were a sword that shone with an unearthly light, a golden chain and a medallion of blue with a jewel-like brilliance.

'The Sword of Destiny,' Conor breathed. 'The golden chain given to the Prince by his majesty King Ferdinand, a blue medallion and the orange tree in our garden. I wonder what happened to the ring?'

'The end of the search,' Kathleen crooned delightedly. Flash cocked her head and gave a little growl of pleasure. Even before they saw the sailor boy, they knew he had come into the hut. He emerged from the shadows, smiling.

'Thank you both for helping me. Long ago, my ship went to the bed of the ocean because no one would come to our aid. Even now, brave men are risking their lives to save another Spanish ship. The circle is complete; the debt is paid.' A gentle sigh like a breath of wind went through the hut. 'Now, at last, I can go home.'

The twins were never sure afterwards if the sailor had actually spoken or if they had imagined the words.

Kathleen felt something brush against her fingers. Light splashed down one wall and across the floor. Light shone through the figure of the sailor boy as he raised the Sword of Destiny in a final salute. Before their eyes, the wooden box was crumbling away. Then, with Kathleen and Flash, the Prince went out into the morning light.

Outside, the sky was growing pearly pink and the island was coming alive. Far away was the first sound of the dawn chorus – faint and thin and wonderfully sweet. Now the wild music was growing stronger and coming nearer and the melody was clear: trills and grace notes and runs, spilling from the throats of larks and blackbirds, linnets and thrushes.

'Listen! They're singing the Spanish song,' Conor said. They paused. Then they turned in the direction of the harbour and saw the Spanish sailor go down the island road before them. Proudly he strode along, with never a limp, and onto a ghostly sailing ship that lay at anchor. Silently, the prow of the ship turned. Graceful and swift,

The Ghostly Spanish Ship

she cut through the waters, and they marvelled at the symmetry of her tall riggings and proud sails, waving in the morning breeze. One moment, the ship was there. The next, she had slipped over the horizon.

Conor let out a deep sigh. 'At last the Spanish sailor has gone home.'

Kathleen smiled. 'I'm glad.'

Flash had been soberly trotting along between them. Now she pointed her head, barked and was gone, racing down to the pier. They could hear the familiar chug-chug of the motorboat coming across the water.

'Big Tom is back,' Kathleen cried, and began to run.

'We're coming,' Conor shouted, easily passing her out. At the landing slip, the Ballad Singer and Big Tom were waiting.

'All's well that ends well,' the Ballad Singer sang out, swinging them down and into the boat. 'We got the crew to safety on the mainland. Your aunt is giving them breakfast and the divers are helping to repair the trawler so that the crew can go back home to Spain.'

'Same as the Spanish sailor,' Conor said, satisfaction oozing from his voice.

'We met him,' Kathleen said.

'You dreamt it all,' Big Tom joked.

Kathleen held out her hand. 'I have the sailor's ring, the one the Infanta of Spain gave him.' It was a beautiful gold ring engraved with a hand holding a heart. 'See the inscription, *No tengo mas que darte.* I have no more to give you.'

'He gave you the ring so that you will never forget

him,' the Ballad Singer told her.

'Conor got nothing,' Kathleen said softly. 'Even the crock of gold is only made of rubber. The leprechauns cheated him in the end.'

'I lost my limp,' Conor said, dancing along, 'and that is better than anything else in the whole wide world.'

Flash thumped her tail and her bark said plainly, 'I helped, didn't I?'

'Indeed and indeed you did,' and the twins bent down and hugged her until she shrugged them off and ran away.

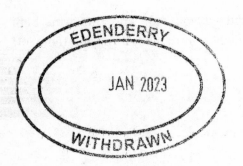